ALSO BY MARY ROBISON

Days

Oh!

An Amateur's Guide to the Night

THESE ARE BORZOI BOOKS,
PUBLISHED IN NEW YORK
BY ALFRED A. KNOPF

BELIEVE THEM

BELIEVE THEM

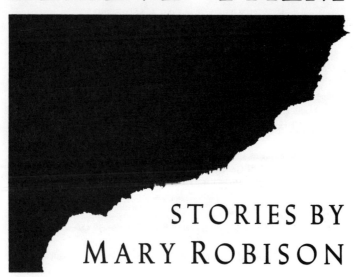

STORIES BY
MARY ROBISON

ALFRED A. KNOPF   NEW YORK   1988

THIS IS A BORZOI BOOK
PUBLISHED BY ALFRED A. KNOPF, INC.

Seven of these stories appeared first in *The New Yorker:* "While Home," "In the
Woods," "Mirror," "I Get By," "Trying," "For Real," and "Seizing Control."
The author is extremely grateful to the magazine for permission to reprint
them.

"Your Errant Mom" appeared first in *Gentlemen's Quarterly.*

"I Get By" appeared also in the 1987 O. Henry Prize Stories collection.

Library of Congress Cataloging-in-Publication Data

Robison, Mary.
Believe them.

I. Title.
PS3568.0317.B4   1988   813'.54   87-82571
ISBN 0-394-53942-7

Manufactured in the United States of America

FIRST EDITION

for Roger

CONTENTS

BELIEVE THEM

.

SEIZING CONTROL

We weren't supposed to stay up all night, but Mother was in the hospital having Jules, and Father was at the hospital waiting.

We spent a long time out in this blizzard. We had the floodlights on out behind the house, and our backyard shadows were mammoth. We kicked a maze—each of us making a path that led to a fort like an igloo we piled up at the center of the maze. We built the fort last, but then nobody wanted to get inside. Hazel patted the fort and said, "Victory!"— from a movie she knew or something. We didn't quit and come in until Sarah, the youngest, was whimpering.

Our cuffs and gloves were stiff and had ice balls crusted on them. Our socks were soaked. All of us had snow in our boots—even Terrence, who had boots with buckles. Zippers were stuck with cold. Our ears burned for a long while after, and our hair was dripping wet from melted snow. We put everything we could fit into the clothes dryer and turned it to roll for an hour.

Our neighbors on both sides had been asked to guard us and watch the house (there were five of us kids, not counting Jules), so when it got late and the TV had signed off we put out the lights and had a fire in the fireplace instead. We didn't subscribe to cable, and Providence, where we lived, has no all-night channel on weekends (this was a Friday). Sometimes we could get Channel 5 from Boston, but not that night, not with the blizzard.

Hazel, who was the oldest of us, was happy about the fire but baffled about the television. Hazel was retarded. She'd get the show listings from the *Providence Journal* and underline what she wanted to see. To do this, she must have had some kind of coding system she'd memorized, because of course she couldn't read. This was the first time Hazel had ever been awake when the TV wasn't.

She watched the fireplace, and once when she saw an upshoot of flame she said, "The blue star!" which was what she called a beautiful blue ring that our mother wore. Hazel watched the fire some more and kept quiet enough. She had her texture board with her on her lap. "Smooth . . . grainy . . . soft," she recited, but just to herself, as she felt the different squares.

Terrence got on the telephone and called up a friend of his—Vic, who'd claimed he always stayed up all night. Terrence couldn't get anyone but Vic's very alarmed parents. He didn't give them his name. Terrence was also drinking a bottle of wine cooler—Father's—which wasn't allowed, but the rest of us had shared a can of beer earlier and now we were having coffee that we'd made in the drip machine, neither of which we were allowed to do, either. We figured we were all about even and no one would tell.

Hazel started to get annoying with her texture board. She had torn off the square of wide-wale corduroy, and she kept wanting the rest of us to feel the beads of rubber cement left on the backing. "Touch this," she said over and over to Willy, our other brother.

We took her to bed, to our parents' king-sized bed—which we thought would be all right this once. And Sarah, the baby,

4

was there in bed already. At first Sarah pretended to be asleep while Hazel was undressing. She could undress herself if she stood before a mirror, and she knew to arch her back and work her hands behind to get her bra unhooked. She never wore clothing that looked retarded. In fact, whenever Father said to her, "How come you always look so pretty?" Hazel really would look pretty. She swung her arms when she walked, the same as the rest of us.

Sarah pretended to wake up suddenly. She wanted her cherry Chap Stick—her lips were so dry, she complained. Terrence must have heard Sarah—we were downstairs—because she was being so insistent. He called, "You left it out in the yard! You had it outside with you. You left it." Sarah believed Terrence, because his voice had authority. He was very attuned to voices, and he knew how to use his though he was only seventeen. He'd say to Hazel, "Don't sound like you're six years old. You're not six." Or if someone said just what was expected and predictable Terrence would ask, "Why should I listen when you're only making noise?"

Sarah wanted us to retrieve her Chap Stick. But the blizzard was still on, and nobody was going back out there, however sorry for her we felt. Most of the time when Sarah was outside, she'd kept her wool muffler over her mouth to protect it. Willy had to wrap it around her, under the hood of her parka, so it was just right. She had baby skin and the cold got to her.

Late in the night, Hazel punched Sarah in the face when they were supposed to be sleeping. Probably they were asleep, and Hazel was probably having a dream. Terrence was interested in dreams and wrote about his in a dream journal he kept. Sometimes he'd ask us questions about ours, or he'd talk to Mother and Father about the meaning of dreams. But he didn't ask Hazel if she was dreaming when she swung and socked Sarah.

We all talked at once: "I can't find a coat. . . . Wear mine. . . . Un unh, I *hate* that coat. . . . This is wet! . . . Go look in the dryer. . . . Get a blanket—get two! . . . No one will see you except maybe the doctor. . . . It makes virtually no *difference* what you're wearing or how you look. . . . Another towel for her nose! . . . Let's just get out of here."

Terrence warmed up the old Granada out on the street, where Father parked it because the driveway was snowed over. We left Hazel alone in our parents' bed, and we carried Sarah. We put her in the back, and then two of us got on either side of her. Sarah was covered up with a blanket and also Father's old topcoat.

The snow blew around in the headlights. No one else was out, and we urged Terrence to run the red lights. He said he couldn't afford to—his license was only a learner's permit. He also had a fake license from one of his friends, but the fake said Terrence was twenty-six, which wasn't believable. We begged him to put on some speed. We said that with a hurt person aboard, the police might even give us an escort through the storm. Terrence said, "Well, I checked her out and she's not that hurt, unfortunately."

A man walking his brown poodle loomed up beside us for a moment. The poodle was jumping around in the deep snow, loving it.

"Dog," Sarah said through her towel bandage. She was wide awake.

After the emergency room, we left Sarah on the car seat. She was out cold from the shot, even though the doctor said it was just to relax her. Her nose was nowhere near broken.

We'd driven awhile and then we hustled into an all-night pancake place, there off Thayer Street. Inside it was steamy and yellow-lit, although it felt a little underheated. We took over one side of an extra-long booth, each of us assuming giant seating space and sprawling convivially. Our arms were spread and they connected us to one another like paper dolls.

We spent time with the menu, reading aloud what side stuff came with the "Wedding Pancake," or with the "Great American-French Toast." Willy wanted a Sliced Turkey Dinner Platter, but Terrence said, "Don't get that. It's frozen. I mean frozen when served, as you're eating and trying to chew." The waitress approached, order pad in hand. She wore a carnation-pink dress for a uniform. We fidgeted in irrelevant ways, as if finding more comfortable spots on the booth seat. But we didn't whisper our orders. We acted important about our need for food. We'd been through an emergency.

After the waitress, we discussed what we'd tell Mother and Father, exactly. They'd be so busy anyway, we said, with baby Jules. They'd been busy already. Father had painted the nursery again, same as he'd done for each of us.

We wondered if washing-machine cold-water soap might remove the bloodstains Sarah had left on the pillowcase.

"We'll tell them . . ." Terrence said, but he couldn't finish. We pressed him. We wanted to know.

"O.K.," he said at last. "We just give them the truth. Describe how we seized control."

We said, "They're going to ask Sarah, and she'll say, 'Ask Hazel.' "

Our parents asked Hazel. She told them everything—all that she knew. She said, "Share. . . . Admit who won. . . . People look different at different ages. . . . Providence is the capital of

Rhode Island. . . . Stand still in line. . . . Mother and Father have been alive a long time. . . . Don't pet strange animals. . . . Get someone to go with you. . . . Hold tight to the bus railing. . . . It is never all right to hit. . . . We have Eastern Standard Time. . . . Put baking soda on your bee stings. . . . Whatever Mother and Father tell you, believe them."

FOR REAL

I was in the dressing rooms, comfortable in my star's chair, a late evening in October. We had taped three shows. My lounge chair was upholstered in citrus-green fabric. My section of the studio dressing rooms was all lollipop colors, in case a Cub Scout troop or something came through.

I was alone, confronting a window. I could see lights around the Dutch Pantry restaurant, and a single truck enduring the horrific eastbound uphill grade on the Pennsylvania Turnpike. Beyond that, the mountains—which were florid in the autumn daylight—had darkened to a hostile black-green, as if they were closed for the night to visitors. Their pointy peaks were brushed with beautiful cloud smoke, though, and on the piece of Lake Doe that I could see, there lay a startling reflection of the night's quarter moon.

I was Boffo, the girl clown, who hosted Channel 22's *Midday Matinee*. We ran old bad movies on the *MM*—or worse: old TV pilot shows we passed off as movies. My job was to ridicule the films and gibe at our sponsors, so the viewers at least would have something to smile about. The job was complicated. I felt tested, whenever the cameras were aimed at me, to improve the little monologues and jokes I had written—to act funny, as if I really was Boffo.

Three years of playing her had told on my face. I used an

9

expensive, hypoallergenic clown white that I special-ordered from Chicago, but my complexion was coarsening. My wigs were coral-pink acrylic, with tubes for hair; I wore a skullcap, under which I had to keep my real hair cropped short—an inch or so at most. The fact was, I never wanted to be a clown. I hadn't gone to clown school in Florida or anything, but I'd studied broadcast journalism here at our own Penn State. I didn't even particularly like circuses. I was pushed into the job by management.

Gradually, two things happened. I stopped feeling so reduced by the clown suit. The first months, putting on the nose and wig and the purple gloves with gigantic gauntlet-style cuffs, I had always winced and apologized repeatedly to myself. I got around that by deciding one day that the suit was only a disguise—something to do with my act, not me. I hadn't invented Boffo or her costume. What else happened was that I became convincing, actually pretty good at playing her. Also, I grabbed a crazy amount of pay.

I came back from the window and tried to call Dieter, using the special oversize clown telephone near my chair. I had to thump the out-call tablet four times, because Channel 22's phone system was no better than its movie library. Arranging the receiver so it didn't touch my greased cheek (I had another show to tape, so I was still in full Boffo gear), I tapped off Dieter's number. In the mirror, my cheek was porous and as white as a sheet of rag paper. While Dieter's telephone rang, I found myself trying to loosen some of the coils in my phone's exaggerated wire cording. I permitted ten rings. No Dieter. *"Wo ist Dieter?"* I asked myself.

Dieter was the only guy I bedded with just then. He was a few years my junior—a recent college grad, in fact—which was part one of the problem. He was employed by the Channel 22 news department. He was all set as long as his student visa remained valid, which it wouldn't for long. Dieter was a

West German citizen, and he was going to get shipped nicely back there soon if he didn't come up with a legal reason to stay.

"So what the goddam hell is this not-there jazz?" I asked in my shrill Boffo voice. I often reverted to character when I was in clown rig. I pretended to abuse the enormous receiver, throttling it before I dropped it back onto its rest. "Dieter is always home *in die Nacht. Nacht* is ven the news happens!"

Dieter wanted to marry me, and plenty of times I had agreed, so he could stay on in the States. But I didn't want to marry Dieter, really, and that was part two of the problem: he knew.

I made fun of him a lot, for being such a tidy person and so formal-acting. He wore starchy white shirts always, with cuff links. The line in his side-parted hair was ever straight. *"Was ist das?"* I would say to him. "Did you use a slide rule and a T-square to get that straight a part? It's centered perfectly over your left eye!" An outsider might think I treated him condescendingly, but I wasn't asking any outsiders.

I plucked up four rubber balls and juggled them. I flapped my Stars and Stripes shoe, as long as a diver's fin, on the tile. I got a rhythm going with the soft pops of the rubber balls and the splat of my shoe. That's what I was doing—that and worrying about Dieter—when Terrence, the floor director, opened the dressing room door and said, "We need you for the spot."

"See the moon?" I asked Terrence.

The spot was a little promo for a coming show. Out in the studio, I stood where they told me to, before Cary Williams's camera. I juggled the balls and kept slapping my shoe.

Terrence said, "Three, two, one," and pointed to me before he was distracted by something happening over his headset. We waited.

I liked Cary Williams, the cameraman. He was in his fifties, dimpled and shy, with an impossible laugh. I said, "Hey, *hi!*—it's Boffo. For tomorrow—whoa, brother. We've got a movie that'll bring up your breakfast, brunch, lunch, *and* dinner. And next you'll get to hear me read a medical review on toxic shock syndrome. Lastly, we'll have a visit from Sam and Janet. Sam and Janet who?"

Pete, who was holding up the cue card, said flatly, "Sam and Janet evening." That was our oldest joke.

"Yeah, yeah, could we just do it right for once?" asked Terrence.

I peeked around the trunk of Cary Williams's camera. He was not even smiling. I said, "If I had to do it right, I'd quit."

I had a pretty comfy condo, with a view of the mountains and Lake Doe. When I was home there, nobody knew I was Boffo the clown. Tonight, because of a flood watch and drenched roads, Dieter was staying over.

I got into bed with him, but also with a vinyl-bound notebook that I balanced against my knees. I tried writing some material—just dumb puns and so on—for a Gregory Peck movie we had scheduled. The film also had Virginia Mayo in it, so I was goofing around with "Ham on rye, Greg, and hold the mayo," and variations of that kind of low-grade snorter.

I couldn't get much written. I was too conscious of Dieter and how much more convenient the future would be if I loved him some, or at all. He was sharp-looking enough—cool-faced, with a romantic broken nose, from being a wrestler for a while in college. He had a slippery grin that was a trick to summon.

"Laugh, Dieter! This is honestly funny, and I'll think more of you," I'd tell him sometimes as he helped me get dressed.

He'd hold up the big stiff costume while I boxed my way into
it. Then he'd steady me, so I could fold myself way over to
strap on the floppy, dazzling shoes.

"Right, *ja*," he'd say, his face entirely sober.

He tried especially hard whenever we watched a taped
Midday Matinee rerun together. But he always failed because
he didn'ᴛ have the same references. At first, I figured I'd just
catch Dieter up—give him the lowdown on somebody like
Charlton Heston and why it was a pleasure to crack on such
a jerk. But that wouldn't have done much good.

Other times, too, Dieter kept missing the jokes. In the
supermarket, when I was helping him shop, he'd look down
and see that I had slipped nine or ten packages of pigs' feet
into the basket. If Dieter knew this was odd, he didn't know
it was funny.

And then, *Dieter* would do things, himself, that to me were
a laugh, but they weren't to him. I mean, I've never been to
West Germany, but there must be less space there. Because
Dieter would go into a coffee shop or someplace like that
and walk right up to a booth where a couple of people were
already sitting, and he'd *join* them. He'd just sit there and read
his newspaper, or he'd start a conversation. I'd hear him calling them *"Meine Herren"* or *"Gnädige Fräulein"*—"Your Lord-
ships" and "Gracious Lady"—and then I'd discover they'd
never met before!

A scary thing about marrying Dieter was that it could
also mean three years of being spied upon. We'd have to be
completely true to each other and very intimate, because I
had heard awful stories of immigration inspectors doing spot
checks, or calling in one member of a couple like us and
asking all manner of personal questions. What's her perfume?
What color towels were in your bathroom this morning? What
was she wearing when she left the house this morning?

I squinted now at Dieter and asked him, "What's my favorite perfume, that you see me putting on all the time?"

He shrugged. He said yellow-colored— *"Gelb."*

"Dieter, that's any or all perfume," I said, and rocked my head on my pillow. "We are doomed!" I threw my Boffo jokes notebook into the corner. *"Ich bin müde,"* I said. "I am ge-sleepy."

I watched through a separation in the draperies while Dieter parallel parked his car in the condo driveport. The wipers quit when he killed the engine. He didn't get out of his car right away, so I waited some more in my foyer. I ended up taking a place on the little settee there, waiting for Dieter to ring my doorbell—after which he would bow and usually shake my hand before he kissed me hello and finally came inside.

Today I rushed him through all that. I pulled his angora scarf away and kissed his throat. I held his rain-chilly face between my hands and kissed him some more, although he hadn't even taken off his perfect topcoat. Today I wasn't going to put up with fussiness. We were going right into action, and this time that would change my heart.

But this was Halloween. Dieter had a gift for me, and, he said, hopeful news. His gift was a gold locket. The locket was pricey, I sensed, but there was no photo. "Hey, it's Claude Rains," I said.

Dieter gave me a tilted head, a curious look. At last he said, *"The Invisible Man?* Because in my locket there is no *Lichtbild*—photograph?"

"Way to go, Dieter! That's exactly correct. How'd you get that?" I clapped him on the back in congratulation.

He also had a box of candy for me. He had signed the card, "On Halloween, to my clown."

I slowed up and made coffee for us. We sat by the fire I had laid earlier. Our view through the bow window at the end of the living room was of mountains and the lake, more brilliant than ever, against an ashy sky.

The fire rustled busily and we sampled some of my chocolates. "So far, I've had bad draws," I said. "A cream thing and an orange center, and now this one is jelly."

Dieter's eyebrows went up. It occurred to me to tell him about Halloween candy: chicken corn and those tiny orange pumpkins. I decided the info wouldn't have much utility. I also wanted to hear Dieter's hopeful news.

It turned out he had been to the lawyers'. There was a chance that Dieter could get a job as a translator for an international news service. He was smart. He could read six or seven languages. The catch would be convincing an immigration inquiry board that he wasn't taking the job away from a qualified American. Dieter said he'd have to prove he was the only person qualified. But I was still bent on seducing Dieter and falling in love with him. I stood him up and kissed him hard, no doubt tasting of raspberry jelly.

I watched the red light on Cary Williams's camera and held for the noise of the five-second buzzer. I had been on the set only an hour and the wig was toasting my scalp. I didn't usually admit this even to myself, since it wasn't a solvable problem. What I did mind was that my cheeks were pasty and stiff because my whiteface had dried to chalk. Like an idiot, I had left my makeup kit in my car trunk overnight. Instead of floods recently, we'd had a snap of fearsome cold —excessive for November. At night, in the car trunk, some of my Boffo cosmetics had actually turned to ice.

The Halloween visit was our last serious get-together, Dieter had announced. He hoped he'd be around town, maybe still be my friend, but he said he couldn't go through with a marriage—because, he said, I *shouldn't*, not out of simple goodwill.

He had asked me a question I couldn't exactly answer: "What if you fall in love with somevun for real?" He said I couldn't be with the hypothetical someone for three long years.

I spoke the movie's lead-in now. The card on Dieter's candy box had said, "To my clown," hadn't it? The few times I had got to Dieter, he had a barking, punctuating laugh that would have been an incentive to me, I guessed, had I heard it more often. It would have helped me be funnier. I probably hadn't been funny lately, I realized, even on Boffo's level, because I'd been shoring up all my energies while I aimed at being a better person than I was.

I interrupted the movie's intro. I said to Cary Williams's camera, "Excuse me, viewers? Ladies and germs? You've been being cheated, in all truth. You've been seeing a lazy job of Boffo. But stay watching. We're about to press the pedal to the floor. We're about to do it right."

On the set there, that got a laugh.

WHILE HOME

The Deforest kids were in the Lakebreeze Laundromat. "Whose treat is lunch?" asked Jonathan. He and little Lana looked over at their older brother, Shane. Severely handsome, he was taking his ease in a shrimp-pink scoop chair. Lana, who was seven, had been lifted up and set on top of a broken clothes washer.

"I guess I'm the only one with money," Shane said morosely.

A machine, beginning its spin cycle, let off a shivery whir.

"Tie my shoe for me," Lana said.

Jonathan, who was eighteen, had already flicked through all five of the laundromat's magazines. He gave up pacing now and drew what string remained of Lana's shoelace back and forth between the lowest eyelets of her sneaker, evening the shredded ends.

"Tight," Lana said.

From his chair, Shane said, "I know who *had* money. The dog. This morning, I found the corner of a ten in its bed, Lana. The rest of the bill obviously chewed up and swallowed."

"No, sir," Lana said. Rosalie was her dog.

"Probably my ten," said Jonathan, as he secured a bowless double knot on Lana's shoe.

"You ate the money, if Rosalie didn't," Shane said to Lana. He sighed. "O.K., I'll cover lunch," he said. "But one of you has to bring it here to me. I'm not sitting in any restaurant in a swimsuit. You've got to go get the food—is that agreed?"

Shane was conscious of his nice good looks and his light voice, which made these orders seem less than demands. He was a sometime model and actor, who had come back for a while to recover from a year and a half of spectacular unsuccess in Los Angeles. If he found a decent job here at home, he might just change his plans. His present role, of returned prodigal and older brother, was the best of his career so far.

"Sure, sure, agreed," Jonathan said.

Their town was Ophelia, Ohio, on the lake. The three of them had been swimming in Erie's friendly little surf. Jonathan's blond hair formed into stiff bunches now as it dried.

"Let's get pizza from Sub Hut," Lana said dreamily.

"Too much salt," Shane said. "I like a subtler pizza." He took a sandwich Baggie, folded many times for waterproofing, from the buttoned pocket just below the waistband of his swim trunks and extracted a twenty-dollar bill.

"Hey!" said Lana, in admiration.

"I'll have a BLT, rings, and a Strawberry Blizzard," Shane said.

"That a regular or a Blizzard Supreme?" Jonathan asked.

"Second one," Shane said. He almost had to shout, because water was firing into a nearby machine.

They had been waiting for their beach things—towels, Levi's, a pullover, and Lana's terry cover-up—to finish in the tumble dryer. They had a clothes washer and dryer at home, on the other side of town, but they were temperamental machines, tricky to operate, and their mother had forbidden their use while she was away. She was in Milwaukee, taking care of their grandmother after an operation. "That means especially Lana," she had said. "No, especially *you*, Jonathan."

Jonathan was on his way out of the laundromat now, but he circled back. "Look outside," he said, and directed Lana to the front bank of windows. "At this man. He's coming by any second. You've got to see this, Shane. It's like his hair was sculpted on. Like it's carved out of wood putty."

"Here he is," Lana said.

"Here, Shane, quick!" Jonathan said. "Is that not carved hair?"

But Shane did not get up. He sat lower in his chair, with his neck bent. He was hugging himself.

"Uh oh. Shane's thinking again," Jonathan said.

"I believe I might be going to have a damned seizure," Shane told them after a moment. "I only said 'might,' so try not to get hysterical."

"Nah, you're not. Are you?" Jonathan said. "Please say no, because I don't remember what to do. Maybe you just have water in your eardrums. I get it every time I swim."

"It's more than that," Shane said.

Lately he had been using a new anticonvulsant for his epilepsy. He had developed an allergy to his regular medication.

Lana kicked the machine beneath her with the heel of one sneaker. "But this is the first time I was allowed out!" she said.

Lana had been confined to the Deforests' front yard for the past couple of weeks. This was for her own good, her mother had reminded Mr. Deforest and the boys before she left, because Lana had recently come home, after an afternoon at the little Kristerson boys' house, with her dress on backward and the buttoning sequence missed by two.

"Please wait until after we eat, and then you can," Lana said to Shane. "You shouldn't lie down here or anything."

"Lana, he can't control *when*," Jonathan said.

Without taking his eyes from the floor tiling, Shane said, "No, and I really think I'm going to."

Back home, Shane rested in a rope hammock that was strung between two sweet-apple trees. He had not had a seizure. "Quit waiting!" he ordered Lana.

She kept watching him. She was lying on her belly on a green upholstered chaise outside the trees' shade. She had stripped down again to her red-checked gingham swimsuit, which she had worn at the lake. "I'm not bothering you," she said.

"You're waiting for me to have a convulsion. If you weren't, you'd be helping Jonathan dig or you'd chase Rosalie. You'd be doing anything but lying still, Lana. I know you."

"I don't care," Lana said.

"Not responsive," said Shane.

"Tomorrow I want to help Jonathan. Today I'm getting more suntan," she said.

Jonathan was on the other side of the modest yard, working a patch of worn lawn with a shovel. Whistling rhythmically to himself, he jimmied loose a stone and then kicked the point of the shovel into the ground again for a new bite of dirt. He was digging a shallow trench around a mound of earth he would eventually dress with rocks—making a strawberry patch, he had announced. His real idea was to strengthen his back and shoulder muscles. He wanted to be able to manage a more serious, faster motocross bike than his aging Suzuki. He had talked this over a few days before with a mechanic at the Cycle Corral—a fellow who had once raced professionally.

"I'd forget about a KTM or a Husky, if I were you," the mechanic had said. "A real thunderbutt bike'd just intimidate you. Way too much power in the midrange, with your little arms. You'd get blasted out of the saddle. See, I could give you this 495 and take your old bike and in the woods I'd still beat you, because you have to stay lower in the power band or lose it. While you're fighting, I'm gone. And you won't want to take a monster bike off to college with you anyway. Not freshman year, you don't."

Jonathan twisted his shovel on a carrotlike section of root he had struck. He chopped at it, rested, and chopped. He looked up as two young women approached the split-rail fence that bordered the yard. The Deforests' neighborhood was old enough to be very shady, but the women were in a stretch of sun at the moment, walking jauntily and seeming carefree and entertained by each other.

"Shane," Jonathan said in a low voice. "Two girls coming."

"Describe them," Shane said without raising his head.

"They look nice. One has sort of beaming red hair. I mean bright-bright."

"It's Kay," Shane said. "A chatterbox and sort of a rival. I don't want to see her. Are you positive they're coming here?"

"They're *here*," Lana said. "Open up your eyes and find out, Shane, instead of always asking Jonathan."

"Can it, Lana. I have a good reason. I can't just gape around at them. I mustn't show interest. Kay works at the store where I've been desperately trying to get a job."

"Well, I'm not here," Jonathan said. "They're your problem, Shane. I'm not talking to them."

Sitting forward in the hammock, Shane said, "Kay—hey, hello."

The girls had stopped, still in the sun. They had roller skates slung around their necks.

"Shane? I remembered your name," the redhead said. She folded her pretty freckled arms on the fence's upper railing and planted a green espadrille on the lower. "And you re-membered mine."

"His name is *what?*" the other girl asked. She was more delicate than Kay, and darker.

"It's Shane. Isn't that cool?" Kay said. "Hey, there, Harpo!" she called to Jonathan.

"He'll never forgive you," Shane said. "He hates his curls."

Jonathan had turned abruptly and was facing in the op-posite direction now, digging away at the already trenched earth.

"That, whose whole life you've just ruined, is my brother Jonathan," Shane said. "This is Lana, my illegitimate child."

Lana made a show of covering herself up to her nose with her beach towel.

"He's joking," the redhead explained. "That's not his kid."

"So let me take a guess where you two are going," Shane said. "I have the gift of sometimes seeing right into the fu-ture. You're on your way to ... to Skateland."

"Astonishing," the red-haired Kay said.

"One of my gifts," Shane said.

"You didn't get the job at Carlton's," Kay said to Shane. "Have they told you yet? They're hiring this other guy."

Shane had met Kay before his interview at Carlton's two days ago. She worked in the ladies' half of the apparel store, which specialized in expensive tailored wear. He had applied for a position as a clerk and salesman. With his modeling history and his looks, he figured he'd be good at fitting and convincing menswear customers, although he had no expe-rience at the work.

"They haven't said anything *official*," Shane said.

"Well, they're not hiring you," Kay said. "Say, I forgot. This is Maria. Remember, I told you about Maria? My friend that lives in the other half of my double? Only she owns, I rent. She's my landlady! Aren't you?" Kay said to Maria.

"It's true, I swear," Maria said. "I'm sorry about it." She patted Kay's arm.

Shane closed his eyes again for a moment, and both girls were instantly quiet, watching his beautiful profile.

Later on in that week, Mr. Deforest sat in his carpeted kitchen, watching TV. He was home on his lunch hour. The air in the kitchen was cool and full of the aroma of the oniony egg salad Mr. Deforest had just prepared.

"Looks good. Thank you and greetings," Shane said, as he entered through the archway. "Now, please, Dad, say only the best things you can think of about my appearance." He was dressed in a poplin suit, a blue shirt, a navy-and-yellow silk tie. He was going to another interview in the afternoon.

"You're good enough for a royal wedding, but you'll have to model somewhere else, honey," Mr. Deforest said. "You're blocking Beirut."

"Dad, this suit failed me once before at a job interview. Does it look cheap or something?" Shane said.

"Affordable, I always say, not cheap. But no. Hell, no, Shane. It's a better summer suit than anything I own. You look like a store-window dummy."

"Maybe that's the trouble." Shane scraped some egg salad from its bowl with the wire whisk and ate very carefully, his head far out over the table.

Lana darted into the room and immediately took her father's lap for a seat. Jonathan came in from the yard, shirtless and newly sunburned. "Surprise, surprise, everybody. Egg salad for lunch," he said, sitting down.

"If you know how to make anything different, I pass the apron to you," said Mr. Deforest. "I'm a genius with thermocouples, but this and potpies are just about it for me and cooking."

Lana was eating handfuls of the salad, straight from the bowl. "Sure hope you washed your hands," her father said.

"A *month* of eggs," Jonathan went on. "Our family cholesterol level must be right off the charts."

"We've had lots of other foods," Lana said. Her face was smeared with mayonnaise.

"I'm seeing this guy today, over in Lorain—a sporting-goods store," Shane said. "My last shot. If he doesn't hire me, I'm closing out my savings and heading back to L.A."

There were groans of protest from the table. "Your mother wanted you around at least until she got back," Mr. Deforest said. "Grandma's getting better every day. Why don't you hang in here a little while?"

"Because it's devouring my pathetic bank account, Dad, and I'm also sponging off you. When I was out on the Coast, I made fun of this place, and now I don't feel good enough for it, since nobody around here will hire me to shine shoes. So to hell with it."

"Will you be in movies?" Lana asked.

"Yes," Shane said absently.

"He really could be. That was next," Jonathan said, more to Shane than anyone else.

The television news ended with an admonition from the anchorwoman: "It's twelve twenty-eight and ninety-four degrees, so have yourselves a record-buster, but take it slow out there. Stay cool."

"Talking directly to you, Jonathan," Mr. Deforest said. "You ought to take some salt pills if you're still going to work on those strawberries."

"Salt pills after this egg salad? I'll be the only teen-ager to die of sodium poisoning," Jonathan said.

An old episode of *Hawaii Five-O* started up, and Mr. Deforest ticked his spoon on the table in rhythm to the show's opening theme. "I wish I could stay for this," he said.

"What's the big deal about ninety-four degrees?" Shane said. "In L.A., that's the norm."

"Well, for June," Jonathan said.

"You'd think it was some *crisis*," Shane said. After a moment, he said, "You know, things were looking up out there. I had a sort of letter of inquiry from the William Morris people after my commercial. That's what hurts. To get turned down here by some pimp in a button-down collar."

"Don't be too hard on your home area," Mr. Deforest said.

"*Will* you be on television, Shane?" Lana asked.

"I already was, Lana. You know about that. And can't you eat with slightly better manners than Rosalie—which you forgot to clean the burrs off," Shane said. "You have to *groom* this sort of dog, Lana."

The chimes of an ice cream truck sounded out on the street. "I hear dessert coming," said Mr. Deforest.

"Quick, Pop, give me money," Lana said, hopping down from his lap.

"We just hoped you'd stay around for the summer, before you go chasing your stars," Mr. Deforest said to Shane, reaching into his pocket.

"It all depends on this job," Shane said.

"I'm sure glad it's not me," Jonathan said. "I might do all right during actual exposure time, during the interview, but right now, beforehand, I'd be throwing up."

It was Sunday. Lana was on the screened porch, fixing round stickers onto her tissue-wrapped gift for her father. The stickers said things like "Grin and Ignore It" and "Things Are Getting Worse—Send Chocolate!"

Shane was lounging on the wicker sofa with a copy of

Variety. He wore a black polo shirt and white trousers today. "Lana, tell me again, did you really check for ticks in your hair?" he asked. "There were three on Rosalie last night."

"Yes, Shane."

The east wall of the porch held tendrils of ivy. Through the ivy and the screen's mesh, out above the trees, the sky looked chalky with clouds. It was much cooler this Father's Day morning.

Jonathan lay in the hammock outside—a curled sleeping bundle. One hand dangled loose, still wearing a cowhide work glove.

The day before, Jonathan had ridden Lana on his Suzuki through a meadow and a shady woods where they knew they'd find butterflies feeding on the wildflowers and among the willow and wild cherry trees. It was Lana's plan to supplement her Father's Day present with a framed specimen. They captured and let go a few cabbage whites and one faded viceroy. Then, in a lucky swoop, Jonathan netted a red-spotted purple. Back home, he chloroformed the butterfly in their killing jar—a thing he had learned in biology class. "It's gone to sleep," he said to Lana.

"He stayed in the hammock last night," Lana said now to Shane. "I had another present for Dad, but Jonathan let it go."

"I know," Shane said.

Jonathan had confided to Shane about pinning the butterfly the evening before, only to find that it wasn't quite dead. Its wings rose and quivered, and now and then beat rapidly enough to make a fluttering noise. Jonathan fled his bedroom, leaving the butterfly impaled, and hadn't yet gone back there. He told Lana he had changed his mind and released their specimen.

"Everything set?" Mr. Deforest yelled to them on the porch.

"Sixty seconds!" Shane called. He collapsed his paper. "Lana, get Jonathan. Those're enough stickers."

Lana went out and returned with Jonathan, who looked sun- and sleep-dazed. He took the seat next to Shane on the wicker sofa.

Mr. Deforest entered with his face bright, his hands folded behind him. "Well, hot ziggetty, a holiday for me. What have we got going here?"

"Cards first," Lana said.

Her father obeyed. "Great card, Shane. Your mother's is nice too—I opened it after breakfast. She asks how you're doing on that new medicine. I'm wondering the same."

"If the moon's full, I grow huge hands and fangs, and hair all over my face, but those are the only side effects so far," Shane said. "I'm settling into it."

"This one, of mine," Lana said.

Mr. Deforest opened Lana's envelope and showed around the contents—a bumper sticker with the message "I Love My Mutt!"

"And if that's not Rosalie's picture on there, I'll eat it with mustard," Mr. Deforest said. "Good for you, Lana girl. This goes right on the car."

"Over my dead corpse," Jonathan whispered to Shane.

Mr. Deforest opened his gift from Lana, saving the wrapper stickers for her. "Lana, you are a shopper! Men's-formula hair spray. I do need this."

Lana took the can from her father and showed him how to work the nozzle.

"Excellent, baby, but not so much on the ivy. The ivy doesn't need it too bad today," Mr. Deforest said.

"Mine," Jonathan said. He reached under the wicker sofa.

Mr. Deforest hefted the big package, wrapped in gold foil. "Is this a joke? It's too big."

"I still had some graduation money and nothing to do with it," Jonathan said.

"Well, you made me look awful," said Shane. "Aside from my card, I didn't do anything. I've been pinching every cent for L.A." He had not been hired by the sporting-goods store.

"Holy mother! Look at this, Shane. Lana, look," Mr. Deforest said. He swept aside tissue wrap.

"Damn, it is nice. Really nice," Shane said. He got to his feet for a closer look.

"Extraordinary. A duffel bag you would call it?" Mr. Deforest said. "Get a load of this leatherwork. A place for socks, toiletries. I got a hundred zippers here."

"Where'd you buy it?" Shane asked.

"Carlton's—before they didn't hire you. Sorry," Jonathan said.

"I thought so," Shane said.

Their father said, "You could put a *suit* in here."

"You wouldn't, though," Shane said. "You'd wear the suit."

"Thank you, Jonathan, thank you," Mr. Deforest said. "Now I have to think of someplace nice enough to go."

"I've got a nice trip all lined up for a bag like that," Shane said. "You wouldn't want to let me break that in for you, would you, Dad?"

"Hint," Mr. Deforest said.

"Are you really going to go?" Jonathan said.

"Yes. I wish I could wait for Mom, but ... I'd sure feel better about myself if I were stepping off the Trailways bus with that bag over my shoulder. I'd send it right back to Dad."

"It would have to be in virgin condition," Mr. Deforest said to Shane.

Shane said, "Well, you know me."

Lana was in the yard now, running with Rosalie and giving off screams.

Jonathan stretched, groaning. "Lana had a butterfly for you, Dad, but I messed it up trying to mount it."

"From the meadow? You check her for ticks?" Mr. Deforest said.

There was a silence on the porch and Shane and Jonathan and Mr. Deforest all looked out at Lana, who had straddled the dog.

"I better rescue Rosalie," Shane said. "Lana still doesn't believe you can't tickle a dog and make it laugh." He pushed the screen door open but then paused and said to Jonathan, "You maybe ought to come to the Coast with me. We could have a wild time."

"Yeah, it'd be fierce," Jonathan said.

"Feelings aren't hurt, are they?" Mr. Deforest said to Jonathan when Shane had gone. "It was your graduation money, I know."

"I can't believe I'd ever pick out anything he'd like so much. That's truly a first," Jonathan said.

"But you wouldn't consider what he said. I mean about going with him. I don't think he meant it literally."

"No, I know he didn't," Jonathan said. "Don't worry, I know."

Mr. Deforest had picked up the bag again and now practiced walking up and down the porch with it. "This is first-class," he said. "You can hang it on your shoulder or carry it by hand." He put it down again and directed a look at Jonathan. "O.K., the truth. You're hurt," he said. "And you want him to stay here, stay home with us."

"Yes, but no—no, I'm really not. There's something else. I have to go up to the bedroom to make sure that butterfly's croaked, once and for all. And throw the damned thing away.

It'll put a couple years on me, so expect an older son to come back down. I'll be about caught up with Shane."

"You might want to rethink," Mr. Deforest said. "Before catching up with Shane. I sort of remember being his age. It was terrible. Maybe just skip it when your turn comes."

YOUR ERRANT MOM

My High School Art Teacher

"So there went Kurt Schwitters's *Merzbau*—an incredible piece of art—devoured by the Nazis. He built another one, also destroyed," said Mr. Lee. We were outside on the grounds of my old school in my home state of North Carolina, where the soil is sandy loam and the state motto is "To Be Rather Than to Seem."

There was a warm crosswind from the sea just over a wall, down from the school grounds, below the baseball diamonds. I said, "That must be like what happened to pointillism. When Seurat died so young, I mean."

"Nope, no parallel," Mr. Lee said. He wasn't a patient man, nor did he have time for expected details. For instance, he was now in need of a haircut. His black-and-white mane flopped left to right in the wind. And he wanted a diet, and a more careful shave.

Over the sea's pounding, I heard one of my twin daughters. She said, "I've been bitten by something. Now I get polio!"

"Malaria, maybe. Not polio," said the other twin.

Mr. Lee was sipping from an aluminum can of Diet Slice.

He fished three neatly folded sheets of paper from his trouser pocket. He opened the pages and said to me, "You know what this is? An essay you once wrote for me. The criticism exercise? I still keep it."

I confided in Mr. Lee about my girls. I said, "The best thing about Hallie's being back from Chapel Hill for the summer is she persuaded Mev to come with her. So I get them both. But now that could go out the window. Mev has been talking to army and navy recruiters."

"You may have the wrong kind of kid," Mr. Lee said.

The twins closed in on us. They wore seersucker shorts, blowing T-shirts. Their heads had crisp blond hair, Peter Pan style—youngish for twenty-one-year-olds. Mev was saying, "It's just a welt, Hallie. A small—it's sort of a big welt."

"Now you've met the twins," I said to Mr. Lee.

I was suddenly overcome with the chills that accompany a serious headache. I was suddenly sick, and I told them so.

"You?" Hallie said. "I'm the one with yellow fever!"

My Birthday Present from My Boyfriend

I turned forty-three, and Devin gave me a white Alfa-Romeo Spider. He took me out to Blackbeard's Galley for supper—a long trek. We rode the car ferry across Pamlico Sound to Ocracoke Island, on the Outer Banks.

I stayed in the Alfa on the ferry. I was savoring the car, and I didn't want to wreck my dinner dress and hair. Devin hung on a rail and watched the sunset playing on the crinkled water.

The light was fading as we entered Blackbeard's—named after the pirate who was captured off Ocracoke by the British and executed. We sat on a plush sofa in front and drank Campari, waiting for our name to be called. The place was in season, bustling. There were antique mahogany furnishings, high ceilings, Waterford chandeliers.

My temples stopped throbbing eventually. They'd been at it for two weeks. And eventually Devin put his chin on his palm and told me about his wife. "She dropped dead the first day of nineteen eighty-four," he said. He smiled. "I had to miss the Rose Bowl Parade."

"What did you think of my daughters, truthfully? Did you like them?" I asked him.

"No."

"Come on," I said. "Didn't you think Mev was funny, telling about—"

"No," Devin said.

"You've got to admit that for their age they are very, very attractive."

"Not to me," Devin said.

"Well, I like them. I was proud of them," I said finally. I was furious with Devin, but I couldn't help smiling about my birthday present.

The Palmetto

A porter in a linen jacket and alligator shoes took care of me on the train. He gave me a newspaper. I read the obits while I ate a raisin Danish. I had brought my own Twinings China Black tea bags. I drank the tea, plain. I had steeped it in Amtrak's pot of boiled water.

"Should've flown," said the dapper man in the seat ahead of me. He had mentioned he was from South America. He was talking to a woman in a suit of twilled silk.

"Are they crossing you up?" the woman asked. Her voice was rich, from deep in her throat.

I listened only selectively to the two of them. I heard the phrases "backup crew on the way ... new people going to make it tough ... kick off a week from tomorrow—no later ... if we plan to get out clean, which we do."

"I must explain," the South American said. He got back all of my attention. I was interested in an explanation.

"Please don't. I don't care," his woman friend said.

"Only take a second," said the South American.

But the cars rattled over bad track and I splashed tea on my newspaper and missed whatever came next.

A Visit from Mick's Folks

Our house was a raised ranch with multiple additions, east of the East Dismal Swamp and west of the Outer Banks—Pea Island, the National Wildlife Refuge, Kill Devil Hills, Kitty Hawk. It was a nice house, a long way from people.

The twins were watching a PBS production of *Francesca da Rimini*. I heard one twin say to our bulldog, "Shut up, hound. Here comes the saddest part."

My husband, Mick, took the dog out onto our front lawn, recently mowed. I followed. He walked with dragging, heartsick steps.

Mick's parents came cruising up the road. They turned onto the snaking line of pavement that was our driveway. I had the Alfa-Romeo parked where they wouldn't see it, behind some prop-rooted mangroves.

Mick smelled of Canoe and he had on a polo shirt—lemon yellow. He pushed up a shoulder of the shirt, threw an arm to wave hello. "This," he said through a gritted-teeth smile, "will be the worst day of our lives—I know, I know. But I wanted them to have a whack at seeing the twins."

His father heaved himself from their car. Nearly seventy, the man was bullish thick. He wore chinos that were flat in the rump. His face was the hue of pie dough. Mick's mother fluttered a hand at us. She was already weeping. She was just as big as her husband.

My High School Art Teacher

Mr. Lee's house was set high on pilings. On the desk in his living room was a Plexiglas box with a collection of fossil casts marked INARTICULATE BRACHIOPODS.

"Don't you hate it when there's both a knock at the door and the phone rings?" Mev said, beside Hallie on the main couch.

"It never happens. So no," Hallie said.

"Does to me," said Mev.

The living room had a lot of black lacquered wood and white leather furniture. There were photographs of faces— very intense—blown up to single-bed size. They hung on three of the walls.

"Aren't you two impressed with this place? How could you not be?" I asked them.

"Sure," Hallie said.

Mr. Lee said, "The trouble is, you bring in a bucket of Colonel Sanders, the whole effect's ruined. Next a Sunday newspaper, a bad pair of bedroom slippers. Horrible. Or your cat drops a Hartz Mountain toy."

The Palmetto

The woman in the silk suit had a good vocabulary, I decided. Her deep, dark voice made a kind of music I didn't have to listen to all the way to appreciate.

The train smelled sweetly of disinfectant. Our seats were swivel loungers, upholstered in red. There were napkins clipped over the fabric of each seat's headrest. The windows were red-curtained, and filtered the dying light so it flattered the passengers.

The sounds kept me awake—the metal door rocking and, from the adjoining club car, splits of champagne being opened and the buzzer for the microwave.

A few passengers were trying to sing the show tune "Once in a Lifetime," and they were trying to stand close together despite the slamming and lurching of the train.

A Visit from Mick's Folks

"Are the twins ready for this?" I asked Mick, too late for him to answer. He threw our bulldog a fluorescent ball. The dog came obediently back to Mick with it. The dog's coat was tawny, brindled.

Mick's dad stepped up to pump my hand. I hugged Mick's mom. "Rough trip, Elise?" I asked her.

"I just cry," she said.

"She cries at the television," said Mick's dad. "At bowling shows."

Hallie came outdoors and Mick's dad called, "There you are. Whichever the hell one you are."

"Sometimes I forget," Hallie said with a tired smile. "Mother? I'm biking into Dunphy for a split second."

"You're not!" said Mick.

"Let her go. She needs some things. She'll be right back," I said.

Hallie spun off on her ten-speed. The bike made the promising ticking noises of time speeded up, of escape.

"Mickey kid, this lawn's a sorry thing," Mick's dad said.

Mick despised the name Mickey. He said, "We're sort of French about that, Dad. We let some of it go on purpose."

"I'd love to weed it, deadhead it for about an afternoon."

"He talks big, but he would drop right over in this humidity," Elise said. Mick's folks were from Michigan, and they did not like our steamy days—my steamy days, my state.

"Sometime, could you show my parents that painting you did?" Mick asked me.

"What painting?"

"The one with the airplane and the Japanese man," Mick said.

"I had to burn it," I said, and acted sad.

My High School Art Teacher

Mr. Lee's telephone was ringing. He said, "Don't answer that, under pain of death." We were headed out back to view his yellow fringed orchids, which were over three feet tall, many of them, and all with spikes of orange flowers.

We stayed on the deck. Mr. Lee asked me to go to his kitchen. He asked me to bring him soda and a whiskey glass and his whiskey, and he told me where I could find everything.

"Children," he was saying to the twins when I returned. He was implying picture frames with his hands for Mev's and Hallie's faces. "My glory, you're good-looking girls!"

I shook my head at him, yes. I had been waiting to hear that.

"Our noses are like doorknobs," Hallie said.

"I think we're fat," Mev said to Hallie.

"Fat kids with doorknob noses!" said Mr. Lee.

"Would you possibly—this is awful—would you maybe have a spare cigarette?" Mev asked him.

He said, "I don't smoke. If you do, at your age, you're an idiot."

"Well, I do," Mev said. "You think your—uh—friend in there would mind if I had one of his menthols?"

"I think I'd ask him," Mr. Lee said.

"I got the habit from studying," Mev said. "And now I've just, you know, got the habit."

"Break it," said Mr. Lee.

With My Car Parked at Devin's

I was thinking it was interesting, and ominous, that the furniture Mick and I had chosen for the raised ranch was expensive, but all of a movable, temporary kind. We had foam flip chairs, lightweight couches without frames, futons instead of beds, many wicker pieces with detachable cushioning. Our shelves and tables could collapse or fold. Things were stackable.

Mick was answering our telephone, telling Devin, "She's not here." Mick said I had gone to Charlotte to negotiate a contract—probably off the top of his head. I owned a gallery over in Raleigh. Our next exhibit of Jim Dine prints was not to be mounted for a week. Our last show was by a local hyperrealist who did gleaming oils of drag-racing cars. Those were just coming down.

"Devin's looking for you," Mick said to me, after he'd hung up the phone.

"Well, I'm not crazy to talk to him," I said.

"Lie away," Mick said, and laughed.

The heavy things in the raised ranch were the paintings crowding the walls. There were so many, and some by big names—an Oldenburg cartoon, a Katz oil, a panel by Helen Frankenthaler.

I said, "Mick, I could lend you twenty thousand, you know. Substantially more, in fact. Painlessly. You could travel. You could set yourself up somewhere pretty nice."

"Me?" Mick said. "You're the one who's leaving, baby."

"If," I said.

"If what? No ifs. My house, you're out."

"If you think you can keep it up," I said.

"Don't judge me by my parents," Mick said. "I can pull my own oars in this world."

Mick either never understood or he never believed how much I liked his parents. Elise was close to loving, whatever that meant anymore. I didn't remember my own mother. Long, long ago she had died.

The Palmetto

The couple ahead of me kept their reading lights on through the night until dawn. I wasn't disturbed, but almost grateful I was awake for the night ride.

I saw, by a linesman's shed, a lot of finely chewed sawdust on the ground. We drove over a gorge on a rickety-seeming trestle. The train was late. The South American man was talking. "Could you please speed it up?" his woman friend asked him.

"Quantico!" our porter called out.

My High School Art Teacher

Mr. Lee was the nearest thing I had to a best friend, but I wanted to shake him now with all the strength in my arms and scream, "Wake up!"

"Don't disturb him. He mustn't be awakened at this time of day. Please. The living room," whispered Mr. Lee's housemate.

We both stared at the sleeping form in the blue wash of light from the bedside clock radio.

The housemate was a thin, neat man in a gauze shirt and straw sandals. There were crow's-feet by his eyes, but he was as soft-haired as a preteen.

We moved out of the bedroom. "You don't know. I have to leave town soon!" I said.

"That may be, but why tell us?" asked the housemate.

"Because. It's necessary to say goodbye to *someone*."

"Look," the housemate said kindly, mildly, in the tones of total understanding. "If it's come down to Lee, you should just go."

A Visit from Mick's Folks

Mick's arms were all chigger-bit. The scent of his cologne seemed so thick now, it renewed my headache.

"Tell the truth. Are the twins going somewhere?" I asked. I had heard their voices, coming animatedly from upstairs.

"You're going somewhere," Mick said.

Our bulldog crept under the dining table, where we were.

The table was a collapsible kind, on casters. The dog was hiding from the beckonings of Mick's mom and dad, who were in the next room, pretending ignorance of us and interest in art magazines.

"Then they'll come with me, and enroll in schools up North," I said.

"They'll visit you up North. Eventually."

Later, before I closed the bedroom door on Mick, he asked, "Why'd you have to take them to Mr. Lee's? Let alone their meeting Devin."

"I figured you'd be hurt. It's too bad you found out," I said. "I just couldn't stop myself from showing them off." I meant *any* of them—Hallie, Mev, Mr. Lee, Devin.

Two Steps Forward, Two Steps Back

The faucets in the new place gave the coldest water I ever felt from a tap. And the rooms were appealing shapes—not all square. Bushes of bittersweet grew like mad against the edifice.

Entertainment most evenings was dancing with Devin to jump versions of old songs. He called me his heart tonight. He used the French word *coeur*.

I watched a Richard Burton movie on the tiny Quasar, had a snack of toast and well-chilled beer. There was a street map for here, wonderfully thorough, that I had scheduled to study. Instead, I chatted with my own twin, Teresa, over the phone. At first, this was punishing for me. My situation revealed failure in at least two of my biggest roles. But Teresa said, "Relax. Modify and revise your plan, is all. You try to be a hundred things, you're bad at all of them, no?"

"Time to learn to swim?" I said, and I could hear her smile

through her answer: "Probably." Between us, learning to swim meant not asking others to buoy us up and keep us safe.

A bronzed reproduction of Degas's *The Spanish Dancer* had arrived at last—a nostalgic doll for me. Also delivered was a photo collage that the twins had made. It had pictures of a living crocodile and the bait shops at Nags Head, and some artsy snapshots of dried swamp grass.

I would sleep on my stomach now, without a pillow, and with no sustained thoughts. I wanted what I wanted. Before bed, I had read stories with I-narrators who could've been me.

TRYING

Friday night, Bridie's rock group were into their second set at the K. of C. dance. They were an all-girl band that went by the name Irish Coffee. They did popular songs and a handful of simple electrified versions of Celtic songs they'd been able to learn.

Some boys in St. Augustine's School jackets crashed the makeshift ticket gate, which was two girls at a card table with a spool of purple tickets and a glass jar of dollar bills. A couple of the boys had beer—bottles of Killian's Red. "You don't want to drink that," Bridie O'Donnell said into the microphone during a break between numbers. "It's made by Coors."

Three of the St. Augustine's School boys moved up front and stood there, facing the stage. They did a prepared jig during the group's next song—a three-chord, just-the-chorus rendition of "The Lads of Bofftae Bay." On the last note—a dominant chord from Karen Jorry's bass guitar—the boys whirled and let their trousers drop.

Some pushing and pulling ensued. Karen Jorry and the group's drummer, Ellen Gautier, left their equipment and stomped off the stage.

At the microphone, Bridie said, "Come on, please. No

43

kicking. You don't need to kill them—just get them to leave. Guys? Take your teensy imaginations out of here." But the shoving went on some more.

"Save my amp from getting knocked over—*that* one, not this one!" Bridie shouted now to Proudbird.

He jumped onto the stage, spun, and crouched. The big amplifier was still attached to its wires, but Proudbird got it up and onto his back.

"What *was* all that stuff—mirth?" Bridie said.

"Yah, I guess mirth, man," Proudbird said. He shrugged under the amplifier.

The two watched as the annoyed dance crowd began to flow out of the K. of C. hall, observed by a brown-uniformed security guard.

Bridie was sitting tilted back on a folding chair, reading a basement-press newspaper she'd smuggled into the convent in a leg of her jeans. It was the day after the K. of C. thing, and she was serving detention for class truancy or some other infraction—she wasn't even sure.

The convent, an ordinary two-story wooden house on the St. Benedict's grounds, was home for a dozen Benedictine nuns. Also on the grounds, in a kind of cluster around the Romanesque cathedral, were the two school buildings, a rectory, and a gymnasium. St. Benedict's was in northern Virginia, not far from D.C.

Today Bridie was supposed to tidy the convent's kitchen and straighten the contents of cabinets and drawers. She'd been told to box up some canned goods that were in grocery sacks dumped in a corner—donations from parishioners for the Afghanistan Alliance.

Proudbird appeared at the kitchen's screen door. He was

carrying a thin branch with a couple of apple blossoms on it. "Hallo," he said to Bridie.

Proudbird was a St. Benedict's senior, an exchange student from Lagos. He lived with the fathers on another part of the grounds. Bridie—she was a day student, who commuted to St. Benedict's on the Metro from Washington—had got to know him gradually, from serving detentions here on Saturdays and after school.

"You driving me home? Will Father Tournier lend you a car?" she asked him. She ground open a can of apricots as she talked. The other cans she'd unbagged were arranged on the long table so they spelled out "X NUKE."

"Oh, sure, I guess," Proudbird said. He brought another young man into view behind the screen. "A surprise for you, man. My brother."

"What do you say?" Bridie said.

"Johnson," said the brother. The three of them beamed.

Bridie was seventeen and still freckle-faced. Her reddish curls were brushed into no specific shape or style. She had a wholesome look she often tried to sabotage. Above her jeans today she wore a T-shirt with a tiny stenciled reproduction of the Bill of Rights on it.

"I'll be damned," Sister Elspeth had said that morning, seeing the shirt. Bridie always reported to her to begin her detentions. Sometimes she automatically turned up at Sister Elspeth's room on Saturday even if she had managed to stay out of trouble for a whole week.

"Killer, huh?" Bridie said. "I can't take full credit, though. My mom ordered this from someplace."

Sister Elspeth had Bridie's homeroom and also her American history class. The nun suffered from giantism. She was six feet eight inches tall. Her hands and feet were absurdly large, and her face was oversized as well. Her expression—

from carrying around such a large mouth and nose and brow, it seemed—was amused as well as tired.

"You want temperance or fortitude? We're still on the cardinal virtues, right?" the nun asked. She always gave Bridie something to contemplate while serving detention.

"Either," Bridie said.

"We'll hold off on fortitude," Sister Elspeth said. "That leaves temperance. That's finding the middle ground—the trick against going to extremes, you know?"

"Not sure I do," said Bridie.

The nun thought a minute. She said, "You've maybe seen a man being very rash, and he seems brave. A general, let's say. A boss. Maybe somebody's father. Instead, with temperance, he goes along steadily but doesn't omit anything that needs to be done."

"Cool. I can get that," Bridie said.

"Can you? It's sort of Aristotelian. But morals have to come before faith or the other theologicals. You could be moral but still not believe in anything, see?"

Bridie said, "Yeah, I learned all that with justice. Remember, I said in class a guy might be cheating his workers, then suddenly give them a Christmas bonus? Before he's charitable, he's got to be just."

"Right," Sister Elspeth said. "Not bad at all." And with a gesture she sent Bridie off to her detention.

Now, a couple of hours later, Sister Elspeth was in the dining room. "Who've you got in there?" she called to Bridie in the kitchen.

Bridie swallowed an apricot half. She said, "There's nobody else, Sister." This was true. Proudbird and his brother had just wandered off over the back lawns. The whole area behind St. Benedict's steep-roofed church—the rectory, the elementary school, Bridie's high school building—looked snowy, it was so littered with apple blossoms.

"Then to whom were you giving that speech a second ago?" the nun asked.

"To me," Bridie said. "I mean, no one. That's how I always talk to myself."

"Yipes," said Sister Elspeth.

In front of the line of mirrors in the third-floor green-tiled girls' room, two sophomores were exchanging space-shuttle jokes. Bridie shoved between them. She said, "Did you read how they're saying that explosion put plutonium into the atmosphere? And it could give cancer to like five billion people?"

"Don't tell them that, O'Donnell. They might believe you," said Tasha.

Bridie said, "That could actually happen sometime—the plutonium?"

"You're always trying to scare us," said one of the sophomores.

"Yeah, who *are* you?" the other girl said. "We'd have heard of something giving people cancer if it was true."

"You go right on believing that," Bridie said. "Sure, they'd have heard," she murmured to herself.

"You slave to style," Bridie said, and touched the single tiger-tooth earring Tasha wore.

Tasha picked up Bridie's handbag and plopped it down again. "Thought you never wore leather," she said.

"I don't. That's from a rubber tree."

"And what's *this?* Where do you get such stuff?" Tasha said. With a fingernail, she ticked the button stuck to the lapel of Bridie's cardigan. The button read WORK BETTER—GO UNION!

"My parents," Bridie said.

"Who are?" asked Tasha.

47

"Saints. I'm being raised by saints. Honestly. I screw up totally on my own, and they punish themselves."

Bridie's hand had been raised a full sixty seconds. Her Latin teacher, Mr. Lefan, shook his head at her: no.

He had his chair turned around and he was straddling it, facing the class. He leaned his arms on the back of the chair and addressed the students in confidential tones. "You've seen art renderings of the Seven Hills—the architecture and the rest. The Roman baths. But what went on behind that spectacular surface, you ask. *Don't* you ask?"

Bridie's hand again went into the air.

"I'm not calling on you, O'Donnell, 'cause you'd filibuster until the bell," Mr. Lefan said.

"*Please* don't," moaned a boy in the front row.

Mr. Lefan said, "Romans were like present-day bulimics, in that they'd overindulge unbelievably. They'd get drunk, stuff themselves. Then they'd deliberately throw up and go right on back to eating."

Bridie stopped hearing him. She laid her head on her oak desktop. She was in the last seat, next to the rear door. She listened instead as the rough-voiced boy in front of her and the girl to his left quietly traded insults.

"Looks excellent," the boy murmured. "Nice to know you can walk into a pharmacy and buy yourself a tan."

"Shut up, troll. Lizard. You tick," the girl said.

Mr. Lefan was printing declensions on the green chalkboard.

Bridie scooted her desk, by inches, toward the open door. She did this most days, and most days she got caught. One time, she'd made it into the hallway unobserved. She had walked around out there in the empty corridor and taken a drink at the water fountain, waiting the time away.

. . .

During lunch recess, Bridie skipped the cafeteria and walked over to the rectory, looking for Proudbird. Sister Hilma opened the door. She wouldn't let Bridie past the foyer without knowing why she was there. Instead of a habit, Sister Hilma wore a blue-flowered homemade dress and a homemade apron. Her glasses had such thick lenses that Bridie couldn't find the woman's eyes to make eye contact.

"I do have a genuine reason," Bridie said. "He promised to tune my guitar."

"Which is where?" asked Sister Hilma.

"Well, I forgot to bring it today. I meant, some other time he'd tune it for me. But I am doing this paper right now, and I have to get information about agricultural practices in Lagos," Bridie said, lying.

Sister Hilma rolled her eyes but gestured Bridie to the kitchen.

Proudbird was broiling hamburgers. Bridie watched while he stacked a platter with the cooked burgers on buns and doused them with sweet-pickle relish and ketchup.

Carrying the platter, he led Bridie up many stairs to a white-walled suite. Johnson was inside, lounging on the over-polished floor before a color Zenith. He was watching *Victory Garden.* "Hallo," he said to Bridie.

There were only a few pieces of furniture. There was a bed with boards instead of springs and a mattress. "You cannot be serious," Bridie said as she sat down beside Proudbird on the boards.

"Oh, all serious," he said, handing out the burgers.

He and Johnson talked back and forth in their complicated language.

Proudbird said, "My brother tells you it's what we like. The beds like this."

"So I guess I believe you," Bridie said. She put her spine against the powdery wall, trying to get her bottom comfortable on the board seat. "No, I don't. You'd have to be cracked to prefer this. It's cement. It's the same as choosing to sleep on the road."

Johnson looked back from the TV and smiled with Proudbird.

Bridie took a little bite of her hamburger. "Food's at least normal," she said. "What other stuff do you like?"

"Good arms. I like a girl with good arms," Proudbird said. He held back a smile. The action made a parenthesis of dimples around his mouth.

Bridie massaged her right elbow. She had removed her cardigan and tied it at her waist, and now she bunched it up behind her to form a pillow against the wall.

"We've been joking you about," Proudbird said.

"This isn't your bed, then? You sleep in a regular bed?"

"That's right."

Bridie asked, "Johnson, is it O.K. being in this country so far? What do you think?"

"Oh, yah, truly," Proudbird said, answering for his brother. "There's no place else."

"Pleased to hear it, I guess," Bridie said. "Since it's my country."

Back at the high school building, Bridie went to the ground-floor washroom. There were a dozen or more girls lined up at the mirror, with more girls waiting in a second row. Bridie used a sink and punched up at the pink-soap dispenser. A couple of girls next to her were sharing the hot-air hand dryer. Another girl peered around at the back of her legs, looking to see if her patterned panty hose had a runner. While looking, she noticed her friend's shoes. "Tell me, Jan, why do you wear clogs so much?" she said. "They're heavy, they're noisy, they're nerdy."

"For the heels," Jan said. "I'm all of five foot one, and we can't wear—you know—heels."

"I want a sheegarette!" said a girl with hairpins clasped between her lips.

Bridie finally got to use the hand dryer. Over the roar of its blower, she heard someone behind a stall door shouting, "Holland—and then London. No Paris. Only we'll probably end up not going now. Say, you know what's written in here? 'Today is tops.' Now, that person thinks small."

Reminded, several girls produced felt pens and began to write on the stall doors and the green wall tiles. At the mirror, girls took turns writing with a wand of mauve-colored lipstick.

Bridie got out her own black marker from her purse. On the face of the hand dryer she wrote "608/256-4146," the telephone number of Nukewatch, copying it from a page in her trig notebook. "Get this down, or memorize it," she announced. "Especially if you're going on a car trip, anyone. Call them if you catch any trucks carrying bombs. Three things you'll need to look for are that the truck'll be led by a couple of courier cars, and they'll be unmarked, but both them and the truck'll have lots of antennae. And the dead giveaway is the truck's license plate. If it begins with *E* that's Department of Energy, and you've got one. It's carrying warheads. Call Nukewatch and say which direction the truck's going in, but don't follow these guys. They don't want to make friends."

"Litzinger!" said a voice. "You're dead if you stole my chem homework."

"I *borrowed* it to copy. I *told* you. I'm giving it right back," answered another voice.

There was a huddle forming around a girl who was holding a small gold-plated drinking flask. "You each get one little sip and that's all," the girl said. "Pure Chivas Regal. I took it off my gramps. It was in a drawer in this little table, right next to his bed?"

"O'Donnell, where're you from?" a girl with seven or eight hair braids said to Bridie.

"D.C., but I can take the subway, which really isn't bad," Bridie said. "My mom went here, so it's—you know. It's like I had to come."

The braided girl said, "If mine sent me this far, just to go to St. Ben's, I'd be like 'Get out of my face.' Are you going with anybody?"

"Uh, not really. No time. I sort of date this black guy who's around."

"Your parents know? They let you?" asked the braided girl.

"My parents wish *I* were black, actually," Bridie said.

"Here, take these. They're making me mean," Bridie said. She gave her box of Junior Mints to Tasha, who sat just to her right. It was last period—American history, with Sister Elspeth.

Bridie felt in her purse for her pack of sugarless gum and found instead a toy whirligig she saved for times when she baby-sat the kids of some of her parents' clients. Her mother and father worked for a storefront firm that practiced poverty law. She found her chewing gum, sneaked a stick to Tasha, and popped a couple into her own mouth. She reached again into her purse and clenched the spring shaft of the toy. The wheel went around, harmless colored sparks flew there inside her purse, and there was a sharp whirring noise.

"A siren? Say a Hail Mary," Sister Elspeth said, glancing up from her lecture page. She went back to reading.

Bridie chomped her gum to softness. She blew a spearmint bubble, breathed it in, and snapped it with her teeth. Immediately she said, "Pardon, Sister."

"You're pardoned. Forgiveness is a duty, not an option for Christians, by the way."

"Rules for everything," Bridie said.

"What say?" asked the nun.

"Agreeing with you, Sister."

The nun returned to President Kennedy and Premier Khrushchev.

Bridie waved her hand, and Tasha gave a low groan.

"What?" Sister Elspeth said.

Bridie said, "The 'We will bury you' line. If you'd read Khrushchev's memoirs, you'll find out that was a faulty translation, not what he meant at all."

A boy named Chadwick raised his hand, and when Sister Elspeth nodded at him he said, "It's in a Sting song, Sister. Sting has lyrics about it."

"I don't *care*. It was a misinterpretation," Bridie said. "Anyone who can read would know that." She snapped her gum again, for emphasis. Some of her classmates tittered.

Sister Elspeth said, "Bridie, I warned you. And the rest of you can stay after school and laugh along with Bridie for ten or fifteen minutes while she does stunts with her gum."

"Aw, don't make them do that," Bridie said.

"Then stand in the corner, O'Donnell. I'm sick of dealing with you. While you're over there, you can count the holes on the cinder block at eye level. The fifth down. Block E-five. I know how many holes it has, so don't try to pull anything."

"Got it," Bridie said. In the corner, she sneaked a look at her wristwatch. The class would go on for another eighteen minutes. There was no hurry yet about counting.

"I'm opening a civics club," Sister Elspeth was saying when Bridie next paid attention. "You're my charter members."

"You're kidding—a *civics* club?" Bridie said to the wall.

"I didn't see your paw in the air to be called on," Sister Elspeth said.

"I'm not being in a civics club," Bridie said, turning around. "That's for the little kids in *Ding Dong School*. You can erase my name—I resign."

"I don't believe it—you're still chewing gum! Take that out of your mouth and stick it to your chin," Sister Elspeth said, getting out of her chair.

There was some laughter, and Bridie grinned.

Sister Elspeth came for the corner, and Bridie gulped and swallowed her gum. She started laughing.

"Stop!" the nun said. "What's the matter?"

"Can't," Bridie said, from behind her open-mouthed smile. She stared up into the enormous face of Sister Elspeth.

"You *have* to," whispered the nun.

"I can't!" Bridie said, and her voice squeaked a little. Her laughter was high and unnatural. Her chest and shoulders shook.

"Please," the nun said. "None of this matters—don't you see? You're acting weird, Bridie. You're scaring me. What's the matter with you?"

Bridie shrugged, still laughing.

Sister Elspeth opened her arms and held them out for Bridie.

Later, when Proudbird was driving her home, Bridie told

him that if she could take some things back in her life, she thought that that would probably be one—the moment she had suddenly stopped laughing and the look of horror on her face that she must have shown as the nun, in huge concern, reached forward to embrace her.

IN THE WOODS

Horses, goes the rap, are skittish and unpredictable and dangerous, but one I knew I got to love, although he was all those things. Sunny, the horse, lived with my sister and brother-in-law on their Indiana farm. A thousand-pound horse of the Tennessee Walking breed, Sunny was a strawberry roan, fifteen hands high. He would let me ride him around the periphery of Kenneth and Barbara's considerable acreage there—hours of riding, every day—and I could safely keep my mind on that, and on Sunny. And I was grateful, because my marriage and most of the rest of me had recently splintered.

It's hard work to ride, and it was usually thick hot weather that summer, yet I never missed a day. I'd gear up in tall black boots, canvas trousers, a velvet helmet. Wearing these clothes every day assured something in me, they were such a treat to wear. From the corrugated-fiberglass stable, we'd go first across a meadow that my brother-in-law, Kenneth, kept mowed. It was washboard earth, ridged and baked hard, and so I'd let Sunny amble. Next we would tour a lane of shade trees and then turn into a careful path that invaded the woods. Along here we'd often get up speed, with the thud of hoof and jingle of bridle and, after a bit, Sunny's rasping huge breath. Deep in, there was a ravine. I liked to rein up on its high side, admiring the frightening detail of full-blown summer. Weed wands would bow to me. Flower spokes would wag, and tree boughs, hideously muscled, would reach for me or shrug indifferently. There were mosses, bright green, and freckled toadstools layered like spills of pancakes against the trunks of trees. Sometimes, over the gabbing and ticking of bugs, I would listen to a tractor's thin ringing. Its noise pulsed every other second, saying nothing, which was best, for there weren't any *words* I wanted to hear.

We'd go on to the open fields, into amazing heat. There were graded and scraped paths there, so Sunny's cannons were safe. I could let him lope. Starting from points between my shoulder blades and breasts, the heat would hold me with its dullness and anger. My focus would soften.

Sunny's scent, I thought, was a regal one—leathery and old. And the heat would draw out other smells around us: cucumber, weeds, and dust. I'd dismount to eat wild scallions, but the blackberry canes that lined one pasture—like rows of spectators for Sunny and me—were so tall that I could pick from them while still in the saddle. Once, while I sat, scrunched in the saddle eating berries out of my juice-stained fingers, there was a weird, thrilling thing. The miserly breeze gave up. I saw total stillness, as in a freeze-frame. It was as though the world had died but not quite yet bothered to topple. Blades of grass, bugs, blank sky, even Sunny, were all cast in glass. I was alone in it and feeling suddenly afloat, as if I had bolted a lot of champagne.

In the weeks before my stay at the farm, I had been awake too much. Whenever I did sleep, what ugly dreams! One I remember was of me roller-skating down cement hill after hill, no way to stop. Marcus, my husband, and I lived in a three-bedroom, all-electric condominium north of Chicago. Marcus, an architect with a pretty good downtown firm, looked as if he could have been my dad or even my grandfather, with his prematurely white hair and silvery beard. Whenever we were in a place where someone might see us together—even if we just stepped out onto our second-floor balcony for a whiff of the morning—Marcus had to have his arm low on the back of my waist, or his hand on the back of my neck, almost in chokehold, announcing to everyone that I was in fact his. To me, that was sadder and a bigger problem than his skirt-chasing.

Evenings on the farm, Kenneth would grill steaks or chops outside and my sister and I would do the salad, sometimes corn. We'd open wine. We would cut up muskmelon. After eating, we'd sit on the long flagstone patio, with its view of yard and pond, and maybe drink a Scotch. One night, we finally talked about Marcus and me.

"You're doing everything wrong," Barbara said, as if she had been holding back for a long time.

"For what it's worth, I agree," Kenneth said.

"You broke a window? You phoned one of these women? Those were stupid moves, honey," my sister said.

"The surest way to drive him off forever," Kenneth said.

"While making anybody else look good," Barbara added.

So I had all that, their opinions, to consider, one afternoon while I was brushing Sunny down, pushing the curry brush along his flanks. Sunny started, kicked back, twisted his great neck, and bit me. Kenneth heard my yelp. He came from the tack room—authoritative in jeans, Dingo boots, a white shirt with pearl snap buttons—and scolded me. "Tie up his lead, for heaven's sake. Get his head up. He doesn't know enough not to hurt you. That's a horse you're playing with, not a puppy dog." And he went on and said I might do well to learn a bit more about barn etiquette before I slapped on Barbara's equestrian clothes and rode out "like Princess Di or somebody."

A week or so before, at the aluminum water trough, I had surprised Kenneth when he wasn't wearing his dentures. Of course I knew Kenneth had been stuck with a removable upper plate for many years, although he was only just over fifty. A truck wreck had knocked most of the teeth out of his teen-age smile. He faced me there at the trough with an unusual gentleness. And then he winked. I made no mention of this to Barbara. Kenneth impatient or Kenneth embarrassed could lose no grace by me—he was tops. He deserved every minute of Barbara, to my mind. He deserved his smart wife and his good farm. Self-absorbed as I was, I had watched him going about the chores of his farmer's life—some piddling, some awful, duties. He labored with a kind of patriotism, as though finishing things and doing them well meant the health of his home, his country.

At the tail of August came a series of savage thunderstorms. The rain flailed in the woods and made Amanda Creek wide. Thunder rolled through the afternoon skies, and lightning whitened the world in strobe flashes. Riding was out. I was talking to Marcus long-distance, in daily sessions—five minutes, then fifteen, finally half an hour—and in our pauses I could hear the crackle of electricity in the lines. When I rang off, I would go stand out in the soupy yard, unsheltered, getting soaked sometimes.

The storms ended in fiery, poignant sunsets. In the blush of one of these, with the frogs and crickets ratcheting away down by the pond, Barbara talked to me. She said, "You know, it's all work. Marriage, money, property—the big things. It's not your fault you're too young to know if it's worth it —seeing to all the details. You've got to—you've got to *insist*."

She was riding in the giant doughnut hole of a tractor tire. The tire was roped to a monster willow, off on the side lawn.

"Or maybe you think there's a simpler way to be. All by

yourself." Barbara was turning the swing in circles, winding up the hemp. "I hear you sobbing into the phone. I know what Marcus is like."

Five days of not riding and I was feeling flabby and earth-bound. In the mirror in the mornings, my hair was very tired, my sunburn drying away and peeling off beneath my eyes.

"Kenneth's cheated on me. I've done it to him. It's terrible," Barbara said. "But being so selfish and wrong often brings with it a sort of strength. You know?"

I knew. That was the look I'd seen in Kenneth's face when I'd seen him with his teeth out. He didn't care.

She raised her anchor foot and let the tire spin. I was dizzy for her. Whatever that moment was in the woods, I wanted it back. I wanted Barbara to stop revolving, and the rain to end, and the summer to start over—for everything to just hold off until I could catch up.

AGAIN, AGAIN, AGAIN

"Miss, start your engine."

"Done," Daphne said. "Now what?"

"You want to shift into reverse, and back slowly to the end of the driveway, and stop."

Daphne swiveled her torso, hooked the white seat back under her elbow, fixed her gaze, and steered with her left hand. She said, "You notice I'm completely turned around in my chair here, one hundred and sixty degrees. Instead of relying on the backing-up mirror, as some people do."

She drove the Saab over a medium-growth shrub and went diagonally across the lawn in front of her house. She dropped the car's rear tires off the grassed curb and braked with a jolt.

"Stop, stop, stop," the man in the passenger seat was saying. "All right, we have a predicament."

Daphne yanked the emergency brake.

"Well done, but that's not a solution," the man said. "And now you've turned on the windshield wipers."

"Then which one again is the radio?"

"You wanted the radio on? We're hanging out in the street, in the wrong lane, going backwards," the man said. He had a shoe-shaped face that was very narrow. His scalp was squared by his brush-cut hair.

Daphne said, "You know, I swear this isn't meant to be

unkind, but you could balance a tray of drinks on your head."

The man said, "No, one can't. I've tried it and it doesn't work."

He swished a long finger into the breast pocket of his summer-suit jacket and came out with a pencil. He took it crosswise into his mouth, like a bit. "You got us into this, miss, now think it through and get us out," he said, with a little tongue difficulty.

Daphne jabbed the gas pedal and the car lunged, engine whining, but was locked by the emergency brake.

"No, not right," the man said. He penciled something down on his tablet of paper.

"Then you drive. This is too hard, and I quit," Daphne said. She climbed from the Saab and walked up the front yard.

She met Coach halfway. He had come from the house, smiling weakly at his daughter. "Very funny. Big riot, Daphne," he said.

"I'm sorry. I know your insurance rates'll be higher and I'm sorry about the yard, but I don't need driving lessons. I already know how to drive!"

The instructor had moved over and was backing the car around, off its curb straddle. He headed for the driveway.

"Is he all right?" Coach asked his daughter.

"By existing standards," she said.

Coach said, "His face is shaped like a goddam shoe."

Coach's family had just moved to the Reed Wilkie neighborhood—their second move in recent years. Coach had roomed at the football offices while waiting for his family and the Mayflower truckload of what they owned.

Coach's last job, where he had logged all winning seasons of his four on the scene, had been the best of his career, and it hadn't surprised him that the Reed Wilkie offer came. He had served as assistant coach for a succession of midwestern colleges. At each place, his position over the team had been more prominent, and his backfield's performance—he was offensive backfield specialist—more spectacular. Now he was Reed Wilkie's head football coach, and the whopping salary he would be paid was, in Coach's view, appropriate. "My fair due," he had said. "Finally."

His wife, Sherry, was in the living room of the new house: a saltbox colonial, set in a bower of hardwood trees. The living room was darkened by mover's crates and boxes. "Good show," she said as Daphne entered.

"Yeah, but I also wanted to kill that lawn jockey, and last night Dad must have slipped out and dug it up," Daphne said.

"He did," Sherry said. She flapped shut her newspaper and squeezed off a new page. She flung the paper open again.

"Is there anything in there?" Daphne asked.

Sherry said, "Of course! The VFW baseball scores, an update on the coming policemen's bull roast, and then a report on the lawn jockey that was found mysteriously in the bottom of the country club's pool. The mayor is quoted here and he says that at first they thought the club's towel boy had committed suicide."

"I hate it here too," Daphne said.

"The main thing is, let's not give it a chance," Sherry said. "Where're you going?"

"Weigh myself," Daphne said.

"O.K., and when you get the results on that, phone them in to this rag. They'll print anything," said her mother.

The bathroom scale was between two Mayflower cartons in the upstairs hallway. There, big August shadows were splashed over the wallpaper. Daphne took off her sandals and Levi's and T-shirt and stood naked on the scale, which was in a pink plastic shell mold. Between Daphne's freckled feet, the dial of numerals swirled. "One hundred big ones!" she called out.

She padded naked around the hallway. The wallpaper had a diamond trellis pattern in rose and teal. In every sixth diamond perched a round-eyed, yellow-horned lark.

When her mother first saw the wallpaper pattern, she had said, "Good. That takes away any temptation I might have to come upstairs here, ever."

"What's so bad?" Coach had asked Sherry. "Birds?"

Daphne had yelled, "An infinite repetition of birds!"

"As if *we're* in a cage, see?" Sherry explained to Coach. "We could spread newspapers on the floor and maybe put down a little pail of water."

"Naw, I don't get that," Coach had said.

From the foot of the stairs now, he called, "Daphne! Get down here."

"You know, rarely is it necessary to shout at me," she called back.

"Come on. We're going driving. Just you—the stunt child —and me," he said.

Daphne was twenty or thirty minutes redressing. She went through six or seven costume variations. She sang vigorously to herself, improvising lyrics to the Stevie Winwood tune "Higher Love." "Bring me a skinnier self! I mean to get thin! I needs to re-duce!"

Finally, she found an outfit she liked, from the deepest reaches of a cardboard transport carton wedged in the door of her still empty closet.

She drove at a speed of ten for the first few blocks. "So we don't crash into this furniture," she told her father. "You notice there are hundreds and thousands of pieces of furniture—see? Sofas? A sideboard? A china cabinet still lined with plates! All along the curb here. We could just come out of our homes, settle into our favorite armchairs, and coexist."

"The Jaycees are having a furniture drive," Coach said.

"Contribute anything of mine you want," Daphne said. "Relieve me of having to unpack. Or dust, later, or scootch things around when I'm vacuuming."

"How come you drive so well?" Coach asked. "Did your mom teach you? You and she probably go joyriding when I'm sound asleep."

"That's right, we do. We put on spike heels and miniskirts over our pajamas, and then we wear blond wigs, and we step out," Daphne said. "Driving is all observation and reflex, Dad. Whoa, I know this guy."

"You would," Coach said.

An emaciated boy with a skinned head stood in his yard. He was pointing a garden hose into the air, writing figure eights and loop shapes with the squirting water.

"He looks so much like the drummer in 'The Music of Church,'" Daphne said.

"I think that too," Coach said. "But *how* do you know him, Daphne? How could you know anybody yet? Is he the—let's see—the owner of the savings bank? The guidance counselor at your new high school?"

"Zinc, hey!" Daphne called to the boy. She eased the Saab to the curb. She said to Coach, "He's just out here whenever I deliver the newspaper. Maybe he has parents, but they stay hidden."

"Hmm," Coach said, and squinted at the approaching boy. "Older, wrinkled versions of him."

"How's your paper girl job?" the boy asked. He leaned on the car and talked past Coach to Daphne.

"Alleged job," Coach said. "She leaves with papers, she returns with none. But what does that prove?"

"This is Coach, my father," Daphne said.

"You're really a coach? O.K., of what?" Zinc said.

"Varsity football. The new head coach of that for Reed Wilkie. And I lecture on history: World Civilization, Greco-Roman Civilization, and one other—they haven't decided," Coach said.

"You never hear much about R.W.'s team," Zinc said. "Sports are kind of low on the totem pole here."

"That's one point of view," said Coach, who hated that the towns and colleges who owned his teams could regard football as unimportant. Coach had worked all along against a morale problem, because his best efforts, and his individual players' best efforts, had usually gone ignored and unrewarded.

Zinc twisted the nozzle on his garden hose, breaking off its spray. He said, "I was a safety, twenty pounds ago."

"High school," Coach said.

"No, sir. Notre Dame. I was deep safety, the last line of defense, until I tore knee cartilage, had arthroscopic, retore the knee. I finally blew it apart, spring training."

"Jesus!" Coach said. "You must have been pretty fast."

"I was fast. I wasn't supersonic. I was quick, O.K.? But not very elegant, I guess."

"Safety doesn't need to be elegant," Coach said. "But he never *ever* better be clumsy. I tell them, 'You ever trip over your own feet, it'll cost everybody!'" As Coach spoke, he smoothed his hair, patted it on top for cowlicks or messed-up places.

"I'm ruined for sports," Zinc said. "I can't even swim. Don't dare lift weights."

"You should be using our whirlpool. We've got every facility over there you could mentally conceive. You want to schedule rehab, I'll see you get access."

Coach extended his hand and shook with Zinc. "Never say never," Coach told him.

Coasting on down the street, Daphne said, "Yimanee! Did you see that? On that porch? Don't be conspicuous, but look back on your side. It's wearing a muumuu."

"I know her. She's out rain or shine. You better back up, so I can say hi."

"Whew!" Daphne said. "For a moment I thought I was hallucinating."

"From that reefer you smoke, Daphne. I've warned you and warned you."

"Hello, remember me?" Coach called to the muscled, heavyweight, suntanned woman. Her dress was leopard print, and her hair was bleached so white it blinked in the light of the late afternoon. She came, nodding, and crouched down to talk to Coach.

"You're the new college coach, from down the street. I'm going to start attending games, being more supportive of the teams," the woman said.

"It's understandable that you haven't," Coach said. "Football's very low on the local totem pole. Sports, in general, are."

"Hey!" the woman said, peering at Daphne. "Aren't you my paper girl? The one with the coppery hair we all call Penny? We know you!"

"Oh, yeah," Daphne said, and grinned. "You all know me."

The woman said, "I should've introduced myself when you first moved in. I should've brought over a pound cake or whatever a good neighbor does. I'm a terrible neighbor."

"No," Coach said.

"I am so. I barely socialize since my Pat died."

"You're a widow, then?"

"For three years," the woman said. "And I don't have a child for company either. Pat wouldn't bring kids into this world. His line was, 'Whatever for? They'll never live to be adults!' "

"It's been nice talking to you, though," Coach said.

"It's gone fast," the woman said.

"Penny here is going to demonstrate her driving savvy on the innerbelt," Coach said, as Daphne shifted out of parking gear.

"Damn," the woman said. "I was about to ask a huge favor."

"Name it," Coach said, and halted Daphne with a hand on her freckled forearm. Daphne shifted back into park. She switched off the Saab's engine.

"You'll have to get out and come in," the woman said. "All it is is I've got an old desk for the Jaycees. Which I can carry; no problem. I just need someone to steer me, especially down the steps."

"I'll carry it," Coach said. "I've had my dose of Doan's." He said to Daphne, "You don't go anywhere."

He vaulted from the car. "She's only got a temp," he explained to the woman, as he reached around to brush off the seat of his sweatpants.

The woman led Coach up onto her crowded porch. He whipped around to check that Daphne hadn't left. She was lounging with her legs stretched over the car seats. Thumping music came from the dashboard's cassette deck.

"I'm sorry, I don't know your name," Coach said to the big woman. He followed her into the dark interior of her house.

. . .

Coach jogged at a loose gait. He wasn't self-conscious when he ran in public, nor did he scowl, as he had seen other runners do.

His new street had old trees, groves of spruce and pine. The houses Coach passed were old models, built before the war, but they had been kept up and cared for without exception. "Small towns!" Coach said aloud. "Who'd live anywhere else? *Why* live anywhere else?"

He passed a dust-colored two-story he particularly liked. The lawn was immaculate, freshly mowed and scrupulously weeded. There were beds of larkspur around the foundation.

A broad-bottomed girl was in the driveway, smearing wax onto the side of a station wagon. She glanced up from her work to smile at Coach.

"Evening," he said to her.

"Go, Griffins," the girl said, and made the number-one gesture at Coach.

He cut across a vacant lot that connected his street to the next. As he trotted, he concentrated on the Green Bay Power Sweep. He said, "Guards pulling and dozing out blockers for a wildly slashing back!" Coach often thought himself to sleep by pretending he was explaining the power sweep—position by position, move by move—to a group who knew nothing about football. He said, "The classic Green Bay Power Sweep is a thing that can be conveyed, a concept that can be actualized, an ideal state with every man doing his job perfectly."

As he ran, he pictured each of his new team's members. He surprised himself by thinking one black kid had beautiful violet eyes. Coach boasted to himself, "They have given me the cream. I have boys digging a *pond* to get in shape for the season."

At his last college, Coach had been asked by Clint Peters,

his tight end, "How do I shake this guy Washington? He's all over me, all the time."

Coach had said, "Get your hands dirty. Try everything. If something works, do it until it stops working."

A miserable-looking dog, walleyed and with a filthy coat, charged Coach now, roaring like a wolf.

"I'm not scared of you," Coach said.

The dog bounded with him, keeping just behind and to Coach's left, snapping for a solid bite of shoe or ankle.

Jerry Wylie, the man who would handle the interior linemen for Coach's squad, watched the dog and Coach as they came running for Wylie's backyard.

"That beast!" Wylie called out.

The dog had nipped from a good angle and bitten the back tendon of Coach's foot. "Yow," Coach said.

"He get you? Keep him entertained!" Wylie said. He dodged into his house. He was out after only a few moments with a Remington twelve-gauge shotgun.

"Get that gun away from here, Jerry. You hear me?" Coach called. He was twenty yards from Jerry Wylie. The dog was huffing and growling. Coach spun on his right foot. He swung his shoe lightly at the dog's face, but missed.

Jerry Wylie braced the shotgun on his shoulder. He was a stiff-backed man with a measly amount of black hair. He squared himself for the recoil. "Stay clear!" he warned.

"Lord in heaven," Coach said.

"He won't feel it," Wylie said.

Coach had a couple of bad helpless seconds before Jerry Wylie screamed, "Kapow!" and fired the shotgun. Coach backpedaled, covered his face with his arms. The blast was repeating painfully in his ears. He could not tell whether the dog had leapt or been thrown, until he saw a divot of turf where the shot had gone into the ground, well behind the dog.

"Object lesson," Wylie said.

The dog was zigzagging crazily, but was physically unhurt.

"I've got steaks going here," Wylie said.

"But what have you got to start my heart pumping again?" Coach said. He entered Wylie's yard.

The screen door sounded, and Jerry Wylie's wife came from the house. Her hair was streaked with blond and she was taller than her husband, made long and stylishly thin. Her legs were bare. She carried a strong-looking drink, the deep orange color of straight bourbon.

"Firing at the neighbor kids some more?" she asked. "Or were there some bumblebees around the rosebushes?"

"That rabid dog," Jerry Wylie said. "Honey, you remember the new head coach, don't you? This is my wife, Carolyn."

Coach got down onto the grass. He embraced his own knees. "She couldn't know me," he said.

"But there you are in your running shorts," Carolyn said.

The yard wasn't a large one. It was bordered on the north by redwood fencing and on the east by a shrub wall. At about the yard's center stood an expensive barbecue cart, smoking with three hearty slabs of spitting flank steak.

"Good to meet you, Mrs. Wylie," Coach said.

"She won't answer to that," Jerry Wylie said.

Coach asked, "She was at the Meet the New Bimbo thing, was she?"

"I'm sorry, I didn't go," Carolyn said. "But you look very good in your nice running shorts."

Wylie had cracked his shotgun apart, and the gunpowder smell mixed with the steak fumes.

Carolyn sidled off toward a crowd of elderberry bushes with fat blooms. A giant butterfly batted around her there. "Here's a monarch, Jerry," she told her husband. "Better get the ammo. You should blow its trespassing brains out."

"Bad marriage?" Coach said.

71

"Horrendous," Jerry Wylie said, nodding. "You wouldn't want to take her too seriously, though."

"Don't worry. Hell, I like her," Coach said.

"You wouldn't want to like her too much," Jerry Wylie said. "She'll sock you in the eye. You care for some brew with this protein?" He referred to the steaks with his gun barrel.

"If you are," Coach said.

Wylie said, "That was salt in that cartridge, was all. I had no real intention of taking the dog's head off. Although the local Humane Society people have been after him for months."

"Why? He's not really rabid, is he?" Coach said.

"No, but he's crafty. He makes jogging or a midnight stroll a living hell. He bites you."

"Tell me about it," Coach said. He used both hands to pry off his Nike running shoe. He tugged down his cotton sock. There was a bloodless pinch mark just behind his anklebone.

"Still, I wouldn't intentionally shoot his head off," Wylie said.

"It wasn't *his* head that concerned me," Coach said.

Wylie took the shotgun into his house. He reappeared eventually with plates, knives, a bundle of green onions. He carried a bottle of Worcestershire sauce under his arm. "You eating?" he asked Carolyn.

She had gone a little farther off. She sipped her whiskey. "Not now I'm not."

"Now or never," Jerry Wylie said. He said to Coach, "I wanted to have German potato salad or a plain garden salad or something with these, you know? But Carolyn wouldn't help me, and I don't do too well with those things myself. But before you complain, remember you're getting five dollars' worth of steak here for the thirty seconds' work you have to do to earn it."

They sat on the grass to eat. Wylie doused his meat with

Worcestershire sauce and alternated bites of steak with chomps of raw green onion.

"Damn good," Coach said. "This is some town. The women are healthy. The roads are clean. The lawns are all mowed. And it's incredible how everyone gets behind something like this Jaycees furniture drive."

"Wait'll you see the turnout for the policemen's bull roast, or what they do for muscular dystrophy on Labor Day. They'll top twenty thousand this year, I'd bet."

"This *meat* is the best thing. At the last place we lived, you couldn't buy good beef. Not for your firstborn could you make a deal for meat like we're having," Coach said.

Carolyn ambled back to them. "Feeding?" she asked.

"Drinking?" Jerry Wylie asked her.

Coach lolled, resting on an elbow. "Carolyn," he said. "You by any chance know a woman who lives down from me? A big, great big, woman who's a widow."

"Her chest," Carolyn said.

Jerry Wylie licked a grease burn on his forefinger. "That one. We don't know her, but we remember her chest. She's outside all year, crushing the springs of that poor porch glider of hers."

"Her breasts are really enormous," Carolyn said. "But everyone says she's disturbed."

"She truly is. Better forget about her," Jerry Wylie said to Coach.

Carolyn disappeared into the house.

"Rest your mind," Coach said. "You couldn't pay me to fool with a sick woman, even if she does have ninety-inch bosoms. Where's this mighty couch we're hauling out? It must be a mother if you can't move it alone."

. . .

Saturday, Jerry Wylie was hunched over in a chair, fore-arms on knees. He had a pudgy cigar fixed in his right hand. His gray eyes were set on Coach.

The football offices were high in a brick building, near a park of evergreen trees, by the stadium.

Coach didn't have to share his spacious room with anyone, and from his windows he could see through the trees to a river with groomed banks.

"The Watertown scrimmage is a problem," Wylie said. "Year in, year out, they stink. Bunch of dogs, Watertown."

"Yeah, but maybe this is their year," Coach said.

"Listen to me," Wylie said. "I hate starting the season with that scrimmage. It's misleading for our people. They begin thinking they're Super Bowl stuff after they paste Watertown, which they can't help but do, because no matter how you cut it, they're playing the Campfire Girls."

"We'll hold it down. We'll keep a lid on it. We just won't build our guys up too much for the scrimmage," Coach said.

It was hot in the office. Both men wore only flannel trunks and rubber thongs.

Wylie seemed to be enjoying himself with his cigar. He used it to make stabbing gestures and to punctuate his con-versational points. He said, "And then after Watertown, oh, boy. Hayes Junior College—H.J.C. God, we wasted them last year. Bud Tipper's their head coach—this whiny guy. After the scrimmage last year, he comes over to Coach Haney—who you replaced—and Tipper says, 'That was un-necessary. That was demoralizing. You have no class, and I am going to remember that last field goal shit.' See, we had scored on them every way you could think of, and with ease. So we decided to try out our field goal procedures, just to see about the snap and so on. And this little nineteen-year-old we got kicks one over the damn bar from forty yards out! Ah, Jesus, we about died. So Tipper, H.J.C.'s coach, says—getting up real close—'You guys are going to hurt sometime for pulling that.' " Wylie pointed his cigar at Coach's chest.

"If you light that whip handle within three miles of this building," Coach said.

"I don't smoke 'em," Wylie said, and grinned.

Coach stood, brushed a drop of sweat from his eyelid. "I'm going to watch the tape of the game again. I bet you don't want to do that with me."

"Naw, I'm going home. Beat the wife, read the funnies," said Wylie. He unfolded himself, and Coach walked him down the hallway. "Soon, scrimmage time. Heads knocking," Wylie said in the way of goodbye.

From the supply office, Coach signed out the black plastic videocassette cartridge and the wide can of eight-millimeter film and the projector—the records of last year's scrimmage with Watertown.

In a tiny, impeccably clean room, Coach plugged in the cassette and sat with his arms folded to watch the color tape as it played on one of the football offices' several mammoth televisions.

Coach watched the patterns of the offense he would control, that he meant to remake, reinvent. "Off tackle, slant, off tackle," he said in disgust. "Haney grinding it out."

Coach's was a wide-open offense, powered by sweeps and quarterback options, and passes off the option. Coach was heavily dependent on the pass. These were not only the tactics Coach preferred, not only the ones he knew, but, he said, "It's what we owe the fans. They didn't come to see mud wrestling." His game had always been to meet the opponents head-on in a blitzkrieg attack, to physically beat and dazzle them. Confusing and dazzling the enemy, confounding with speed and sleight of hand, then pounding them on the ground—these were the methods of balanced football.

Still, last year's players looked splendid as they ran their formations out in slow motion. Everything they did worked; even bungled plays sometimes broke, sometimes turned into long-yardage gainers.

"Waffles!" Coach shouted, not knowing if anyone was home. He slugged his gym bag onto the kitchen counter, which was already heaped with cleaning fluids and rags, fresh shelf liner in cellophane rolls, tissue-wrapped plates and drinking glasses.

"Coming," said Sherry's voice from another downstairs room. Coach couldn't tell which room in particular.

He rooted through packaging, and an unfamiliar cabinet, and, last, a utensils drawer. He gathered a big mixing bowl, a whisk, a spatula, Bisquick. He made batter and poured a puddle onto a Teflon-coated waffle iron that he'd plugged in and brought to full heat. He started a coil burner on the electric stove at the kitchen's center. He flicked on the intensity light and the odors fan in the stove's ceiling-dropped hood. He was peeling bacon strips into a skillet when Daphne arrived at the back door.

"Aha!" she said. "I was right, as always."

"Shut the door, Daph. You'll let flies in. What were you right about?"

"That Mom wouldn't be here, so you'd be fixing some in-between-meal snack," said Daphne. She stood next to Coach at the stove. She picked up a two-tined fork and straightened his bacon pieces for him.

"I am so here!" Sherry said, appearing behind Daphne at the kitchen's entranceway.

"Holy Christ!" Daphne said.

"Daphne, do you have to say 'Christ' all the time?" Coach asked.

"Nope, not all the time. Only when Mom sneaks up behind me. Only when she floods my system with massive amounts of adrenaline."

"Name me a time when I'm not here," Sherry said. She circled the kitchen, tidying up. She tossed out a punctured, emptied V-8 juice can. She used paper towels to wipe a long tearlike dribble of waffle batter from the face of a cabinet.

Daphne had wandered with her fork to the kitchen's back door and was watching out the newly repaned window with its tape and chalk marks. "Still there," she said. "This stray dog that's mooching around on the steps. He followed me all the way home." Daphne had come from swimming at the college's natatorium. Her red hair was still damp, hanging in ringlets.

"Walleyed? Yeah, I know him," Coach said. "You should let him inside, for protective custody. Everybody in this neighborhood's after his ass."

"Maybe when I'm through eating," Daphne said.

"Want to come see my bedroom?" Sherry asked Coach.

"So you did that? Made a room up for yourself down here," he said.

Daphne said, "Separate bedrooms? Uh oh. Time to write 'Dear Abby,' Dad."

"Butt out, Daphne. It's nothing like that," Sherry said. "Coach and I have different needs, different schedules, for one."

Daphne's head tilted, skeptically.

Sherry said, "I tend to get a second wind, late at night, and when I do, I require a work area. I have ideas I have to put to paper, sometimes occurring at three a.m. I want to work guiltlessly."

Sherry was an amateur sculptor and painter.

"Food first," Coach said. "Then you give me the tour."

Coach stepped over Daphne, who lay flat on her stomach on the living room carpeting. She tangled her feet and ankles as she whispered into the telephone. "*My* last incarnation, I know for certain I was a bird," she said.

"Sign off," Coach told her out of habit.

He entered Sherry's new room. It had glossy flooring and powdery walls. On one wall were Sherry's many sketches, pushpinned in orderly rows. Sherry had done dozens and dozens of charcoal drawings on newsprint—possible designs for sculptures she hoped to create. Coach's nose twitched at the oppressive smell of spray fixative.

In one corner of the room stood Sherry's in-progress sculpture pieces. This was where she now knelt, over three assemblages. She was coating their sides and surfaces with wide brushfalls of black goop.

The room's double windows, which were uncurtained and pushed open, let in quadrangles of light, and air that was dancing with lint and dust spores. There were sounds from tennis games being played out on the campus courts, a field behind the house—noises of balls clopping, shouts, yelps, even foot patter.

The long room had a new white cotton rug over its floor's center. On the daybed were a white piqué comforter and large foam-filled pillows of orange and cerulean blue. There were a few ceramic ashtrays placed about. "You smoke all of a sudden?" Coach asked.

"Honey, I made those. They're for decor," Sherry said.

Coach raised his eyebrows as he perused the room. "You are set! This is a full-fledged artist's den!" he told her.

"Thank you," Sherry said.

Coach used the adjoining washroom. He fingered the new puffy towels. He opened the mirror door on the medicine cabinet and saw a toothbrush, still sealed in its plastic casing. There were a matching cup and soap dish with an unboxed bar of glycerin soap, and also a grainy soap, for work-dirtied hands.

"Yep, a bona fide crash pad!" Coach said as he emerged.

"Oops, I nearly forgot. This came for you in this morning's mail." Sherry plucked an envelope from the pocket of her smock. She handed the envelope to Coach. It was blue, with a drawing of a martini-drinking circus clown. "Addressed to you," she said, and shrugged.

Coach ripped loose and scanned the notecard. "Bogus, hogus, dogus," he recited.

"Say again?" Sherry said.

"O.K., I'm quoting. Word for word," Coach said. He read, " 'It's a harvest bash! Yessiree!' This is all in a balloon, like a comic strip, coming from this drunk clown's mouth, as if he's announcing it. 'Where? At Wendy Vicker's, one seventy Red Cedar Lane. When?' The *clown's* asking the questions, right before he gives the answers. 'September second, eight o'clock, or thereabouts. B.Y.O.B.? If you please!' "

"Am I going?" Sherry asked. "Not if they chloroform me and try to drag my comatose body."

Coach said, "And there's a postscript. 'Want to meet your wife and show you off to my group—alternatives to the neighborhood personnel.' And then she signs it, and adds, 'Bring the little copper coin!' "

"Which is code for what? She wants you to pay?" Sherry asked.

"It's a nickname for Daphne. I guess they all call her Penny, because of her hair."

"No. No one's that stupid. Not even here," Sherry said, and whapped at one of her sculptures with the paintbrush. "I will kill and strangle anyone who calls my daughter Penny."

"Easy, easy," Coach said. "Wendy Vicker is just some poor thing from down the street. I moved a piece of furniture for her. She's as friendly as a retriever dog, and built like a goddam Turkish wrestler."

"Oh, I know who you mean. Her?" Sherry said. "She's always on the swing outside her house? She has the largest breasts I've ever seen on a human."

"You mean Wendy," Daphne said, in the doorway. "She's made simple newspaper delivery a hell on this earth. Every day, she interrogates me. She wants every bit of info on you, Dad. No stone is to be left unturned. She's about guessed your hat size."

"Hell, let's *attend* her harvest party," Coach said. "There'll be many young men afoot for you, Daph. And that'll occupy your mom, worrying. Then, while you're both distracted, I'll get big Wendy all to myself. I'll let her pick me up and throw me."

"Dad, I have to tell you, that kind of base trashy humor brings me down," Daphne said. "Wendy Vicker isn't a well woman."

Sherry wrapped her paintbrush in a rag. She said, "Have some perspective, Daph. To Coach, this woman's a final opportunity, a last encounter, an Everest, before he loses his figure and goes to fat."

"This bod? Never happen," Coach said.

He was giving his face close consideration at the half wall of mirror in the master bathroom. Holding his chin thoughtfully in hand, he swiveled his face for both profiles. Age had dropped his browline some. There were white hairs in his eyebrows and a few in his thick head of hair. But his gaze was hard and had purpose. He could focus tightly with only a subtle squint.

He listened now as the TV in the bedroom picked up a preseason pro football game. One of the show's announcers was saying, "Harper's just a rookie, but watch him catch this one in traffic. Then he puts on a little juke, and oh, brother! He turns on the afterburners! He is gone."

Coach hurried into the bedroom. He saw the color commentator for the broadcast saying, "And Bobby Harper has been by no means their only deep threat today."

"No indeed, no," said the play-by-play announcer. "Because although Kip Tandy is hurting, his contribution already this afternoon has been awesome."

"Tandy *is* awesome," Coach said.

The TV guy said, "My oh my, can he ever put a hit on you!"

"He can hit you hard, he can diagnose plays, he has a lot of savvy."

"But that is not true. That is horseshit," Coach said. "He thinks like a truck. He *is* a truck."

Coach went back to the bathroom. "Poor la homo," he said, reading the glossy box that held his bottle of aftershave cologne. He filled his cupped palm with the liquid. Aftershave reminded him of dates—haircuts, corsages, picking up the rented tux, dancing with a girl after the game, live brass music, dancing when he was rib-sore and kicked, his throat strained from celebrating. And how the gymnasium floor smelled of epoxy and varnish, and his father would have to drive him home.

The stray dog, whom Coach had let inside and upstairs with him, came into the bathroom to see what Coach was doing, and if there was anything to hunt down or eat.

The dog leapt high at Coach's side and Coach asked, "You

want me to pick you up?" He hefted the dog and held him a moment for their mirror reflection. "Wants to be tall, same as anything," Coach said.

From the television, there was a promotion ad for a new spaceman series. Coach let the dog down, as a TV actor said, "With you, human, we have no quarrel."

Coach plugged in his shaver's coil of electric wire. He swabbed the razor over his thrust-out jaw, bracing his chin in his hand.

On the television, a play was in progress when the broadcast resumed. The announcer was saying, "He's at the twenty-five, the thirty, the forty!"

Coach left his vibrating razor and rushed for the bedroom. The dog went along. Coach bow-tied his voluminous white terry-cloth robe and pointed at the TV screen. "Did *you* make that happen?" he asked the dog, who tilted up his face and whomped his tail in apology.

"You're O.K., relax," Coach said. "Watch this replay. Keep your butt low. Bah! Interference on twenty-one. That *was* interference. Show the replay again. See him push? Number twenty-one?"

The dog bounded onto the king-sized bed and put his triangular head on a pillow sham. His eyes were pleading with Coach, like a pointy-faced lover.

"Just throw the goddam ball," Coach told the TV.

At halftime, Coach finished shaving. He straightened the shag floor mat beneath him. He tidied the candy-striped shower curtain. He reordered his bottles—shampoo, liquid soap, facial astringent—in their wire caddy. He rehung his soap-on-a-rope from the showerhead. In a strong falsetto, he sang, "R-E-S-P-E-C-T! That is what it *means* to me!" He fed a little water to the potted aspidistra he'd put on the bathroom's windowsill.

From the cabinet beneath the sink, he grabbed a can of

Comet. "Bombs away," he said. He sprinkled the cleanser evenly over the base of the bathtub, making parallel lines of green powder.

At the mirror, he examined his face again. He was always a little tanned or wind-chapped, ruddy from being outside so much. "I look like a duke," he said. "You know what I look like? The third Irish Duke of Earl at his country estate for dove shooting."

He was dressed, standing now before the TV.

The telephones all around the house sounded, but were caught in their primal burst by an eager Daphne. "Someone for you, Dad!" she called. "Can you take it up there?"

Coach said, "Fourth and two, fourth quarter, tie game. Cheese and fucking crackers."

On the telephone was Jerry Wylie. "Partner, I need a bunkhouse for tonight. I've got a lot of other options, though, so if it's inconvenient, forget I asked."

"Here? Oh, sure, Jerry. Hell, you're welcome here anytime."

"Really? You're the closest, is the only reason I called you first. I have plenty of other places I could go instead."

"No, no. Stay here, of course," Coach said.

"Yeah? You got any brew? We could look over some stuff and maybe finally settle on a lineup. Who's gonna be a red shirt finally, and who a white. Settle that for once and for all, if you want."

"Finally," Coach said.

"Or we could nail ourselves to the tube."

"We'll do both," Coach said.

He dropped onto the king-sized bed with the dog, and together they watched the TV. "This was a good game for once," Coach said.

"Come on," he told the dog, and led him downstairs to set him free.

. . .

Wylie arrived with a grocery sack of garden-grown zucchini and tomatoes. Coach asked no questions, at least for the first hour. He and Wylie worked on the squad's platoon assignments. Together, they drafted a tentative lineup for Monday's opening day of practice.

Coach called Red Lisle and David Kull, the two other assistants, to get their official approval. Next he called his trainer, an affable student with dental braces, and read him the final listing. Coach had the trainer write down the list and read it back. The trainer promised to post lineup sheets on the doors of the team's weight room and their whirlpool bath.

Coach left Wylie alone in the kitchen and went up to the bedroom to check on Sherry. She had agreed to spend this one night upstairs so that Wylie could have her studio room.

Sherry was under blankets but seated, with a square wooden drawing board on her lap. She was shading a sketch with a lead pencil, and looked up with an expression of mild impatience. "Why's he here anyway?" she asked, whispering. "Wife on a bender?"

"Don't know, but remember he'll *be* here," Coach said. Sherry often wandered at night. She would awaken, throw back the covers, and stumble from bed. "Intermission," Coach would say, if he too was awake. "Going on your break now."

As he came back downstairs, he found Daphne in the living room, sprawled before the television. He stopped for a moment and watched with her as Madonna cavorted in a music video. "Good, Daphne," Coach said. "Someone for you to emulate."

"Cover your fanny," he told the singer.

He rejoined Wylie, who was beaming over the papers on the kitchen table, his bullet-shaped head in his hands.

"Goddam, this is a load off!" Wylie said. "You know, I've

been looking at the recruiters' scouting reports on our line-men. Did you know that nice kid Francis, the one with the wide ass? Did you know he was sent to Springer Hill when he was *twelve* for beating the stuffing out of his old man?"

"Your kind of hog," Coach said.

"We'll get him a leash and a muzzle," Wylie said. He drank his beer in one tip of the can. His eyes watered and reddened. He screwed the empty can into a crude ball and fired it into the rubber trash barrel.

Coach swirled one of the kitchen chairs around and hung on it backward. "I had a kid once who blinded our manager in one eye—that kind of player, with that much viciousness inside him."

"What do you mean, blinded?" Wylie asked.

"I mean took off his bucket and hit the manager so hard he knocked the guy cold and snapped an optic nerve."

Wylie said, "I'd have had that kid's ass. I'd have it framed, behind glass, hanging on my den wall."

"Oh, he went straight to jail," Coach said. "But back to what I was saying. A guy that mean, that twisted, will give you one or two super games and be so unbelievably good for a while that you'll think you can't win without him. And then he'll go rotten and screw up when you need him most."

"Yeah, the whole thing's consistency," Wylie said, in the tired tones of someone repeating a tired truth.

"You want to eat another beer?" Coach asked.

"Maybe one more," Wylie said.

When Wylie had swallowed another Rolling Rock, he got out a short cigar and nibbled on it, staring ahead. He spoke, nodding occasionally. "Carolyn, my wife. Breakfast the other day, she started talking about you. A lot, in fact," he said.

"That O.K.?"

"That she likes you? Oh, sure. She's got emotional problems, is what gets her going on somebody. She'll like you, and you'll like her just fine, until suddenly for no reason you can think of—when you haven't *done* anything—she'll go and tear up something valued of yours and curse you all to hell."

"Did she do that to you?"

"Something like that," Wylie said.

Coach got out of his chair and stepped into the living room to make sure Daphne wasn't listening. Wylie followed.

"My Lord, she's a good-looking kid," Wylie said as they were observing Daphne.

Coach shook his head yes, and no. "Shh. You compliment her, she'll come in here with us," he whispered.

They reentered the kitchen. Wylie stumbled over the little landing and clamped his front teeth on his cigar. He spat, flung the broken remains into the trash barrel. They sat again and Wylie fingered his way into a box of macaroons that was out open on the table. He held a cookie up to Coach, eyebrows raised in the offering.

"Nah," Coach said.

"So, Francis," Wylie said between chews. "He, too, will be dangerous to society someday. But he'll be fun to coach in the meantime."

It was five-thirty in the morning, the second day of practice sessions. Already it was hot outside. Coach's heart was banging from the cold shower he'd taken. He was dressed in locker room grays and an adjustable acrylic maroon baseball hat.

In the kitchen, he mixed instant coffee crystals with steaming tap water. He was sipping from his mug when Jerry Wylie's car horn blew.

They drove to the football offices. A ground fog, unsteady and white, drifted over the beaten earth of the practice fields. Boys—hunched in pain, limping, not talking—were arriving on foot and on bicycles. No player was allowed to be driven or to drive to summer practice.

These two-a-day sessions were hard on even the best athletes in the best condition. Yesterday a few freshmen had come for work a little out of shape. "Summer fat," Coach had said. Those freshmen had suffered. Just the running had left them wheezing and giggling with pain.

This morning the locker room was relatively quiet. A radio's songs tinkled and some boys were talking, but the ebullient din of yesterday's first practice—the shuffling and punching and grabbing of clothes—had tuned down.

"Folks are hurting," Wylie said.

A few boys in underwear sat up on tables and watched one another's ankles being taped by the trainer. One young man was having the blisters on the soles of his feet painted with yellow Calloustick. All over, the potent wintergreen smell of analgesic balm was mixing with the healthier odor of human sweat.

Danny Colbourne, Coach's star halfback and the player Coach thought his most promising, was shirtless now and looking sinewy as he fussed over his girdlelike hip pads.

"Today we get tough, right?" Wylie asked.

Coach said, "Today, we go root-hoggy die. Yesterday? That was a warm-up drill."

At six-thirty there was a hasty meeting of the whole coaching staff. By seven o'clock—with the temperature at eighty and the humidity woolen, oppressive, itchy—the squad was on the fields.

There was to be no contact during this first week of practices, although the team wore pads and helmets. There were miles to run, wind sprints, laps, patterns for the backs and ends, gutbusters for the linemen.

Coach stood off a little from the doings. His arms were folded and his legs were spread. His mouth was grim, his eyes narrow with concentration.

Jerry Wylie had Francis, who'd proved the ablest lineman, doing penance for messing up on a play. Following each chirp of Wylie's metal whistle, Francis hit the hard grassless earth, did a push-up, sprang to his feet, and, clicking in his equipment, ran in place until the next whistle signal.

"Higher, higher, higher! Get your knees up, Francis. Hit your *chest* with your knees," Wylie barked. He sounded the whistle. Francis went down on his back for five sit-ups, and jumped up again for more running in place.

When Coach had Wylie aside, he said, "Just remember, Jerry, we don't want to get Francis too mad at us."

"I'm not afraid of him," Wylie said.

"Well, *I* sure as hell am," Coach said. He called out, "Gather up red shirts!"

The order went around, shouts of "Red shirts!"

Sore boys came dragging at Coach, their sides heaving. This was his number-one offense, and seeing them, Coach could've choked with pride and power. They circled around, all aching and all trying not to show it. Danny Colbourne had a jaunty expression, but his hands were gripping his rib cage.

For an hour, the offense ran plays. There was no defense. This was a kind of rehearsal, like blocking a stage drama. Coach would bodily move his players. "Munson, you take two steps left, like this: one, two. You turn. And if you see a hole open up, you make your fake, like this, see? You go right through that hole—*right* through. And if there's anybody gets in front of you, what do you do?"

"Take his head off."

"That's correct, Munson. You bulldoze over him and then you bring me his head."

At ten o'clock, after more wind sprints and laps, everybody went inside to shower and eat what lunch he could stomach. There was serious classroom work—watching films and learning the playbook—until one. At one, real practice began.

Daphne was on the window seat in her bedroom, blowing marijuana smoke at the branches of a black-walnut tree. The tree was her view and her camouflage. Chipmunks were squirting around and shivering on the tree's kinked branches.

Daphne exhaled out the open window, and said to a chipmunk, "Hey, fatty."

She took a stick of eye-shadow crayon into the hallway. She colored one of the wallpaper's larks a vivid green.

From downstairs, the bell chimed for the front door.

Daphne stopped coloring and smiled. "I'll go answer that bell, and I'll talk to whoever it tolls for. I'll find out what they want," she said.

Through the foglike mesh of the screen door, Daphne could see a tall woman with auburn hair. The woman held a hand on her chest. She said, "Ah, hello?"

Daphne grinned at the woman.

"Do I have spaghetti all over me? Why are you smiling so hard?"

"Hi. How are you doing?" Daphne asked, a beat behind.

"You're the daughter," the woman said.

"I am the daughter, and Mom—or the wife, however you choose to look at it—is viewing a film." In the background, voices sounded from the living room TV.

"I do hear John Garfield," the woman said.

"He's with Mom," said Daphne.

The woman smiled, a little sideways. Her mouth was large and clean of lipstick. In one hand she clutched a purse that matched her summer shift. She seemed drunk, and Daphne said, "Groggy, but precise. Like it's every day for you. And *all* day, am I right?"

The woman asked, "And are you just high? Or are you a beaming moron?"

"Both, I'm both," Daphne said. "John Garfield! And then another one I love is Ronald Colman."

"O.K., Ronald Colman," the woman said. She leaned on the doorframe.

Sherry came up behind Daphne, saying, "Honey! Whom do you have *captured* on our porch? You're Carolyn Wylie, aren't you? Coach warned me you were gorgeous."

" 'Were' is the verb of choice," Carolyn said.

"You know what I mean. I'm Sherry, the wife. Just knock down the gypsy here and come inside."

"Relax, Mom," Daphne said.

Carolyn said, "The gypsy was just trying to establish a rapport."

"Daphne, this is Jerry Wylie's wife, Carolyn. He's your father's line coach?" Sherry said.

The three moved through the foyer, on into the undecorated living room. Carolyn toppled onto the sofa. She used her toes to pry off her flat shoes.

"Go do something," Sherry told Daphne.

Sherry made a long throwing gesture and said to Carolyn Wylie, "This'll be the living room, once we're rid of these boxes and we've unpacked enough to start actual living."

"Don't count on that here," Carolyn said. "I've been in this town for four or five thousand years, and there's nothing you'd call actual living."

Daphne had stayed and was still grinning helplessly. She said to Carolyn Wylie, "I'm sorry. I know I'm staring. But you are sort of pretty in a ruined way."

Sherry said, "Goddam it, Daphne. Run for your life."

"It's all right," Carolyn said. "She puts a lot of demands on a person's tolerance, but despite that and all appearances, she seems all right."

"Not exactly," Daphne said, and giggled.

"May I have a drink?" asked Carolyn.

"Hmm. We only have brandy, I'm afraid. Some Christmas gift in one of those horrific holiday cartons, so I keep it hidden," Sherry said.

"Ladies, it's much too early for brandy," Daphne said.

"The hell it is," Carolyn said. "Noon's come and gone."

"Damn straight," Sherry said, and bustled off purposefully.

"You get high all the time?" Carolyn asked Daphne.

"Compulsitory," Daphne said.

"I'm nobody's judge," said Carolyn.

"I heard this was a liberal town," Daphne said.

"Oh, yes, liberal. Funded by all kinds of strange pockets, deep pockets. Still managing to harvest the fruits of the industrial revolution—the Bessemer process, the discovery of aluminum."

Sherry arrived back with a tumbler of brandy in each hand. The closing theme for *Daughters Courageous* issued from the big television.

"So," Daphne said. "Are there very many Jewish people here?"

"Seven," Carolyn Wylie said.

Coach was nervous about his quarterback, Michael Lineweaver. The boy was moody, erratic, aloof; a city kid from east New Jersey. He looked too lean and pale to command the other ten, heartier members of the offense, especially the fullback, who was a ferocious kid with a warrior charge, nick-named Stingray.

Lineweaver sat on his helmet now, brooding. He wore a checked half-shirt over his pads. The checks signaled that he was too special a property to be put at injury risk in just a practice session.

"Michael, come here," Coach called to him. The quarter-back came.

"Bring your bucket!" Coach said.

Michael Lineweaver returned for his helmet.

Behind them, the first-string offense, all in red sleeveless half-shirts, were repeatedly running a pass play, without a pass or even a ball.

"What's wrong with you?" Coach asked.

"I's just concentrating," Lineweaver said.

"We're ready for you, we think. You want to take some snaps from Ahern?"

"We been doing that, so we got it down," said Line-weaver.

Coach shrugged.

Lineweaver stuck on his gold-painted helmet. He wore it tipped back on his forehead, with the chin strap and mouth guard dangling.

Ahern, the team's center, placed the huddle ten yards back from the ball by raising his beefy arm into the air. The offense closed into a neat circle. Their backs were bent. Their hands were on their padded knees.

Michael Lineweaver slipped onto one calf to address them. He said, "This is fifty-seven right, H-pass, Bronco on two. Move the ball, strike quick, just like we been doing it in the other sessions. Piece of pie, do it right. Thinking all the time. Break."

The huddle broke up. The players spun smartly away and took their assigned stances along or behind the line of scrimmage. The team was poised now, tense, coiled.

Lineweaver moseyed up behind the line of his troops, almost bored, almost shambling. He flicked his fingers on his tongue, looked quickly right and left over the helmets ahead of him. He scanned an imaginary defense. He settled into a crouch behind Ahern, shoved his hands at the center, and roared, "Seventy-three, ninety-seven, left, dog, hut! Hut! Left, hut!"

Lineweaver had good lungs. On his second "hut," the play exploded, crazily, it seemed at first.

Danny Colbourne pounded along behind the linemen and spurted through a hole made by the left-end tackle. Colbourne ran a diagonal course for twenty yards.

Coach watched Lineweaver, who—after faking a handoff to Stingray—backpedaled four graceful steps and set up. The ball flashed in a whirling motion from Lineweaver's right hand and buzzed, torpedo straight, and struck Danny Colbourne just over the heart. Colbourne folded himself around the ball, and with his legs kicking high, ran free.

Coach worked the chewing gum in his mouth. The gum had gone mostly dry. He glanced at Jerry Wylie, who was bellowing. When Wylie quieted down, he grinned back at Coach and said, "Well, at least we can do *that* right."

"Looked O.K. For beginners," Coach said. To his players, he shouted, "Again, again."

Sherry and Carolyn Wylie were still drinking and chatting in the dim living room. They had allowed Daphne to stay, after she promised, "I'll be quiet. Any assertions that do slip out'll be complimentary. I'm nobody's judge."

The sun had moved and was angling now through the Pella windows, throwing splinters and slivers and puzzle pieces of radiance onto the walls and carpeting of the unassembled room.

Coach arrived home. He was shirtless, wearing only his gray sweatpants and sunglasses he had bought from a cardboard display stand at the Pennzoil station.

"Wowie, zowie," Carolyn Wylie said to him in greeting.

"I was just with your husband," Coach said. He lowered himself into a plastic-sheathed armchair. "After today, we concluded there's no way we can lose a single goddam game. Not with the people they've given us."

"You look great too," Carolyn said.

"I do?" Coach asked, confused. "I need to shower and whatall."

"You could get your hair skinned," Daphne said.

"Are you all drinking that Christmas brandy?" Coach asked them.

Sherry said, "Yes. Why? We are. Daphne isn't, of course. Why?"

"It's just that I saw the bottle out in the kitchen, and then you all seem so congenial," he said.

"He means slatternly. He's talking about me," Carolyn Wylie said.

"Don't be paranoid," Daphne told her.

"Hey, kid," Coach said to his daughter.

"Hi, Dad. You could skin your hair like Zinc's."

"That's one suggestion," Coach said. "So we have a boy from Taft High, in Ohio. And this man—I am not bullshitting—can bench press four hundred pounds, and he can pass by anything on the field. It'd take a combat tank on caterpillar tread to stop him. This boy they call Stingray."

Sherry sipped her brandy. She said, "Has anyone read the new Updike?"

"You three have so much fun being yourselves, all by yourselves," Carolyn Wylie said.

"No we don't. Not fun. Believe me," Sherry said.

"Sometimes yes, though," said Daphne. She was grinning again, specifically at Coach. "You need less hair, Dad," she said.

"All in good time," Coach said, nodding.

CULPABILITY

Jay said over the telephone that he was staying at the Rip Van Dam in downtown Saratoga. He said he was spending and winning a great deal of money on the horses. This was race season. Jay said that from his room at the Rip he could hear the charge bugle at post time.

And he told me he'd left Lyla.

It wasn't much of a decision to cut work to go see Jay, even though my car was in the shop. I called a cab, right away.

I waited in drizzle outside my place. I lived on the sixth floor of what you might call a small warehouse, and what the owners called condominiums. Mine was in a conversion state. My rooms were cleared of rubble. They were wired and had plumbing, and I had made a start on decor. I'd hung sewn things on the white walls—minitapestries, pot holders, a robe.

A sopped collie dog came now and stood under my umbrella with me, waiting for the cab.

On the ride up Route 9, I cranked down the cab's stubborn passenger window, smelled wet evergreen and pine. A ground mist was rising from the warm August rain. Cars had on their fog lights—smeared suns in all directions.

The road became Lake Avenue. I saw a drenched girl trying to pull along a drunk sailor who was draped around her. A vendor was holding tongs by the track entrance, selling steaming pretzels and coffee from under his cart's striped awning. On Broadway's sidewalk, I saw a woman in a business suit and a clear slicker over that who was skillfully steering her bicycle through the morning's pedestrian rush.

The cab dropped me at the Rip, but I walked down to an old-fashioned pharmacy instead of going straight into the hotel. I checked my reflection in the pharmacy's pane window: saw me and the three glass urns of colored water which were the display.

I thought about Jay's phone voice; its mild, somehow sexy pitch and timbre. He had begun carefully, but soon his sentences were spilling out, tumbling over one another. I had heard that pushed sound before, more than a decade ago, when Jay went into an institution the first time. I had felt grown up visiting Jay then, and now I *was* grown up. I was older and heavier. The blunt-cut hair, the big imported raincoat, the umber cheek lines I had marked on my face—none of them really concealed my size and shape.

That first time, Jay had healed and been well enough to make it through grad school. He and I got through together. Now he was slipping and leaving Lyla and I was fat.

In his third-floor room, I found Jay pillowed up on the bed, drinking Bombay gin from the bottle, watching Mary Steenburgen on HBO. I didn't dare take Jay's offer of a morning snort, because my breakfast had been a Little Debbie peanut butter finger (what I tended to eat), and it was only ninethirty, and one sip of gin would have laid me out flat.

I could sometimes forget how physically appealing Jay was. He was lean, had tan and wavy hair, and now, at thirty-five, his eyes crinkled when he smiled. He was prettier than I, even exhausted as he was; disordered, debauched. The left seam of his cotton broadcloth shirt was so torn, the sleeve looked about ready to fall off.

One time, Jay and I had walked by a table of maybe eight

women. They were lunching at an outdoor café. And Jay, in skimpy tennis whites, had—by merely smiling at the women—drawn their unanimous applause. It could be a trial or a privilege, going places with him.

"Hey, Faith. Look what I found for you," Jay said now, and vaulted from the wide hotel bed to search his several duffels. He came up with an volume of Claude Lévi-Strauss's *The Origin of Table Manners*. In grad school, Jay and I had studied structural anthropology.

"I found the best bookstore," Jay said. "Somehow, that is signed."

"My God, it is," I said. "You are smart about gifts, Jay."

Jay was smart about gifts. Over the years, the things he had given me were actually too good. To match their standard, I would have—for example—had to throw out all that I called my wardrobe and start over with the jacket Jay had brought for me from Italy. A chair he once presented me with so shamed my other furniture that I bought drop cloths and cloaked every single piece but the pine and tube-steel and leather Jay chair. Now a signed hardbound Lévi-Strauss would sit on a shelf with my cracked and fading paperbacks.

Back on the bed, Jay told me, "I love my wife, whatever's happening. We go on and off. But it's funny, Faith, how with you things stay the same. My feelings are always the same."

The disclosure more pressed than pleased me.

Saturday night, I drove my neighbor's Hyundai over to Troy, to Lyla's. For a lot of reasons, I didn't phone ahead.

After I knocked on the front door and waited a bit, I was challenged by an inside voice.

"Lyla, it's Faith!" I called, and I heard bolts banging and locks being undone.

My first thought on seeing Lyla was that the hem of her skirt was hanging all wrong and her face was too full. When we hugged, I realized she was six or seven months pregnant. Jay hadn't said anything about that.

Lyla took me into the kitchen, where George was at the stove. George was thirteen or so, Jay and Lyla's boy. He was stirring a big caldron in which he had a pair of blue jeans. There was a lot of Jay in the lanky way George stood, and in his sunny hair.

I said, "Another way to shrink and fade those, so they look more authentically beaten up, is to wear them in the bathtub a few times, then sandpaper the seat and knees."

"You're a friend of Dad's?" George asked. He apparently didn't recognize the fat me.

"Boiling clothes," I said, and smiled. "That I remember. You know, every culture processes *food* by some way of cooking, although boiling's kind of low-order. Roasting would be the aristocratic thing."

"You're a friend of Dad's," George said.

"She's known Jay very well, for a very long time," said Lyla.

"And I know your mother, of course. And you," I said, but in too twinky a voice for a thirteen-year-old, and George sneered at me.

Lyla and I sat opposite at the circular kitchen table. We talked familiarly enough, in familiar fragments, while George was there. We said how wearying my job was. I worked for the government; for the Department of Welfare, specifically. I was a caseworker at offices in what you might call a ghetto.

George poured out his jeans, finally, and left them to soak in cold water in one of the sinks.

As quickly as George exited, Uncle Ajax appeared. This was Lyla's house, which she owned, but her uncle had always lived with her. He was seventy, a retired accountant, trying to be an artist now. He wore his usual garb of paint-stained workman's grays.

He pointed at something outside the kitchen window, and he said to me with some urgency, "Make a wish! Make a wish, Faith!" because, I guessed, he'd seen a falling star.

"O.K.," I said. "I wish ... What do I wish? That I were thirty pounds thinner."

"You're no bean pole," Uncle Ajax said. He squatted low and brought from a cabinet a cold chisel, finishing nails, carriage bolts, and a drill. He put all those back, and got out an armload of spine-marked library books.

"What're those?" Lyla asked him.

"Library books," Uncle Ajax said.

I interrupted with a thing I thought important. Jay had given me an envelope containing a letter written on the Rip Van Dam's complimentary stationery to pass along to Lyla.

She tore the letter out and read. She said, "Oh, listen to Jay apologize! 'I would tell you how sorry I am, Lyla, but why would you believe me? I am terribly, terribly sorry.' And his *t*'s in 'terribly' are those annoying little star shapes."

"What's Jay sorry for?" I asked.

"You're as exasperating as he is," Lyla said. She wadded up the letter and its envelope, whapped them at the wastebasket, but missed.

"Hey, don't," Uncle Ajax said. "We're trying to save paper, remember?"

"Are we? Why? I've forgotten," Lyla said.

"Papier-mâché, starting the fireplace, stuffing our shoes! What difference does it make? We're *saving*."

I cut in on them again, to say I'd been insensitive. "Jay left you, and you're pregnant," I said. "What could he do worse?"

Uncle Ajax gathered his library books. He flipped open the door to the basement he used for an art studio and pitched each book down the stairs. He said, "There're several opinions on what Jay could've done. Mine and Lyla's and now *yours* don't match."

I knew the basement rooms. I had spent many pleasant hours down there the spring before.

Uncle Ajax had put up counters and shelves all around. He kept sixty yards of canvas, five hundred tubes of Winsor & Newton oil colors, tissue-wrapped spikes of vine charcoal, his chalks, his crayons, pads and pads of layout paper. He had mammoth stretchers, which were hand built, reinforced, tacked with canvas. They were big enough for larger-than-life portraits of men on horseback. He had a hot plate, with a stew pot where he'd mix his sizing with a wooden paddle, and he'd coat his canvases until they glowed.

March weekends, I had driven down here so Jay and I could serve as life models for Uncle Ajax. We had posed nude, seated side by side, on metal folding chairs before a chrome yellow curtain.

Lyla was out then, usually. George was always out. I had weighed less.

Lyla addressed me firmly now, saying, "Faith, it's like this—"

I didn't let her continue. I said, "To me, Jay seems completely—well, ninety-nine percent—normal."

"He is," Lyla said. "But if he plays sick, he keeps his dignity. How can I argue?"

"I don't know," I said. "If it were me, I'd at least get myself over there."

"And then what? Besides, I used to like Saratoga. I don't want it ruined for me. Remember when the band was still together? Jay and Mack and them?"

I sang, " 'We made such a mess. You screamed no, I screamed yes.' Could've been yesterday."

"It's been two years," Lyla said.

"Two and a half," said I.

"So. Why'd you take it upon yourself to visit Jay?" Lyla asked me.

"Do you mind my visiting him?"

"I wouldn't mention it if I didn't, Faith. He's my husband. It'd help me to know where you stand."

"All right, that I can tell you," I said.

"Yeah," Lyla said. "You'd better not, though."

Jay and I were in the hotel's carpeted lobby, filling an ice bucket from the cooler and getting cans of soda from the dispenser machine. Jay was smiling again for some reason, showing off his dimples.

Two chambermaids passed us, pushing upright Eureka vacuum cleaners. One chambermaid said, "Race you, Dora. Winner gets him, loser has to distract his girlie."

Probably I didn't look like much in the way of competition. The boxy jacket and the capri pants I wore were both mistakes. I had copied the idea of them from a fashion magazine. But my calves bulged where the pants legs ended. And on me, a huge coat was just a huge coat, deceiving no one. I decided it was time for advice from a consultant. I decided no, it was time for a season at fat camp, and *then* the consultant.

Back in Jay's room, I said, "About Lyla ..." I had set myself the task of explaining her to him. "Do you want to talk at all?"

"Well, no," Jay said.

"I'll listen," I said.

"Then maybe the point is what do you need to hear, Faith?"

I said, "It's simply that I have to figure a way to go between. From here to there, without hurting anyone. So you two can get back together, and I can stay your best friend."

"A bad plan," Jay said.

"Why's that?"

"Because Lyla and I can never get back together."

"Baloney," I said, as Jay crossed the room. He fiddled fretfully with the controls on the air-cooling system there, working compulsively and for too long a time.

When he faced me again, he said, "Lyla's trouble. Stay far away from her. I already know someone whose car she threw rocks at."

Jay had a Skidmore degree in broadcast journalism, and he worked as a newscaster for one of Saratoga's radio stations. He often reported about domestic violence, but I was sure he had no hard firsthand knowledge of it. As I saw it, Jay never got a chance to spend much of the hectic imagination he had. He kept gathering more and more information and getting more and more confused about what was true.

He was taking things off the surface of the bed now—a tidy stack of racing forms; the tip sheet, *The Saratogian*; the orderly array of his grooming things: his badger-bristle brush, Caswell-Massey hand lotion, a teensy cloth shoe buffer.

Now Jay was on the bed. He arched forward, took off the jacket of his buff-colored summer suit, next the torn shirt. He was barechested, insinuating, saying, "Faith, Faith . . ."

No question, I would have lunged for him, but there came pounding on the hallway door, and a man's voice yelling what sounded like threats and insults in some foreign language.

"What did you do?" I whispered, terrified, to Jay.

"That I don't know," he said.

I ordered him to hide in the bathroom. When he was out of sight, I opened the door partway on Mack Armbruster, who said, "Hi ya, Faith," and grinned.

"How did you find us? Or, I mean, how did you know Jay was here?" I asked.

"Lyla told me," Mack said. "Only because I'm still Jay's friend."

I warned Mack: "Don't try to talk to him about Lyla. Even if you get what seems like the perfect opportunity."

I was relieved and happy to see Mack, and suddenly resentful toward Jay. I could picture him calmly seated on the bathtub's ledge, reading a racing form.

"You were yelling what? In what tongue?" I asked Mack.

"A joke, Faith. It's how me and Jay announce ourselves whenever one of us is holed up, having a psychotic break. Look, are you or aren't you going to let me in? I have a phone call to make."

I left the door ajar as Mack passed me. At the telephone, he dialed time and weather, I saw. He was faking a pretty convincing conversation with a sex-talk service when I realized that Jay had emerged and was standing beside me.

"You're not hiding well," I said to him.

Mack hung up the phone. He said, "Let's get out of here. When was the last time you ate a meal, Jay?"

"Uh, yesterday. Poached eggs at that pink Mexican place across the street. But there's something I'd rather do. I'd rather you two accompanied me to the track. There's a horse I'm going to make money on." Jay had put his broadcloth shirt back on. As he spoke, the sleeve finally pulled loose and fell down his bicep.

"Some people," Mack said, shaking his head and helping Jay out of the ruined shirt, "should not be allowed to drink."

"Or we could go have my blood checked at the emergency room. I keep thinking I have hepatitis or mono," Jay said.

"The track," said Mack Armbruster.

Mack called for a taxi from one of the phone boxes on Broadway. While we waited, he sang an Al Jarreau song from start to finish.

Our cabbie headed out Lake Avenue. We three were crowded up on the back seat, with Jay in the middle, and Jay swiveled his head from Mack to me, trying to persuade us to pool our moneys and put it on a gelding name Venus.

I said I wanted to be dropped off at my condo, that horse bets were something I couldn't afford.

"Oh, can it, Faith," said Mack Armbruster. "Everybody knows you still have a savings fund from all the dough Jay gave you for writing his master's thesis."

I did not admit this but neither did I say it was untrue. Jay was carefully telling the cabdriver where to drop me.

For the rest of the ride, I had to hear the two of them play their favorite game of trading absolutes.

"Never get rocked on Sun Country wine cooler. It's basically a bad deal. Never watch *The 700 Club*," Jay said.

"Lazy. You have to try harder," Mack said. "Never wear clothes decorated with depictions of U.S. Presidents."

"Never sit on a Greyhound bus next to a harmonica-playing cowboy," Jay said.

I later saw video footage of the day's horse races. They were called by a man in a gabardine suit, with tinted hair, who shouted into a silver microphone. The gelding, Venus, won big.

Within the week, in my repaired Ford, I drove to Troy to see Lyla.

Hers was a great brick residence, on a shady lawn, with a two-car garage in back. I was noticing, from our wrought-iron chairs on the side porch, that Lyla had a BMW so new it still wore temporary tags.

Lyla had gone through business school and was doing remarkably well as a corporate consultant. She had told me she needed a four-door car to impress clients, to get them and things in and out with ease. Also, Lyla said that I didn't understand credit. She said owing forty thousand on plastic made her more valuable. I knew this was probably true for Lyla, and that she'd end up getting paid for owing. Pregnancy aside, it was harder and harder to sympathize with her little bad moods.

"Why don't you go someplace new for supper—like Japan?" I snapped at her.

We had been playing canasta, and drinking from a gallon pitcher of iced Cutty Sark and Coke (a mixture I think had originated with Mack Armbruster).

"Shuffle the cards, Lyla," I said drunkenly.

"No, you do it," she said. "My hands are wet from pouring."

Uncle Ajax had banged past earlier on some painter's errand, talking to himself as he went. He appeared now with silverware, plates, and a three-layer spice cake he'd made from scratch.

"Fairy art racketeers," he said.

"Are they giving you trouble?" Lyla asked.

"You decide," Uncle Ajax said. "I have to chew these Tylenol caplets." He was speaking around a mouthful of something.

He offered me a huge amount of cake; a slice about the size of a hardback book.

"Thanks, but I'm trying to stay away from sugar," I said.

"Oh, me too. Except natural brown, of course, and then

only heaped on peach cobbler." He gave me the plate of cake, and took a seat at the porch table with us.

Lyla said, "Want to tell us why you slept out in the hammock last night?"

"Because it was two hundred thirty-eight degrees in the attic," Uncle Ajax said. "So it was the yard, or put a mattress down in front of the opened refrigerator."

"You've done that. He's done that," Lyla said to me.

"You surely can afford air conditioning!" I said.

They gave me tired looks. "We have air conditioning. That engine you hear is air conditioning," Uncle Ajax said.

I shrugged and glanced off. Across the street, a kitten was smoothing its hind end on the rubber quills of a motorcycle's fresh front tire.

"Storm coming," said Uncle Ajax.

"Storm?" I said, peering around. A sheen had set up on the startling green lawn.

"No," Lyla said, and pointed up to tan and purple thunderheads that mixed and turned silently above us. The sun streaks on the lawn gleamed from the west, where the sky was clear.

"Your neighbors," I said. "I can never tell if they're having a party, or what's just their regular life. How many people live there?"

Lyla said, "You're drunk, so this is probably a waste of an anecdote, but at their last party, an all-nighter ... Wait; I wasn't invited to their last party. I was the only person on the block not invited. Anyway, at their party before last, I was introduced to this politician. Why am I telling you this?" Lyla asked me.

I halted the question with an open palm, and borrowed a line from Jay. I said, "Maybe more to the point is that I *need* to hear it."

"Not that, but this," Uncle Ajax said, and Lyla and I turned to him. He said, "Mack Armbruster. A divinity school dropout. Conscientious in fits and starts. A rich man's son, now a music-business magnate. Now a father-to-be."

"Armbruster?" I said. "Mack?"

"Uh, not cool, Uncle," Lyla said.

I complimented George on the paint-store hat he was wearing.

"Yeah," he said. "I was in buying wall paint. I decided I didn't like the ocher color of my bedroom that much." He pitched the hat over the weed field we were treading.

"Where're we going?" I asked him.

"A place I know. You'll see when we get there," George said.

We passed a trailer park. There were no trees or shrubs. George stomped on one trailer's water hose. It was limp from lying in the sun all morning and was splitting along the seam. He walked ahead of me, and boarded a cadmium red scooter, which he drove into a puddle that was rainbowed with oil. I jogged to catch up.

We went under a rope of triangular flags and crossed onto a highway that was jammed with cars. George pounded the tail end of a halted Toyota. He yelped, dove for the pavement, and gripped his collarbone, pretending injury. He was crying bitterly when the Toyota's driver got out. George yelled at the driver and poked her enormous chest.

I waited on the other side of the road. When George came, he had removed his T-shirt and was blotting his real tears with it. George's naked chest was a version of Jay's chest.

George led me into a construction site that smelled of new

tar. There were stacks of drywall board about, and dozens of crunched soda cans. There was a boy George's age, named Walter Green.

"You can call her Faith," George told the boy. "But don't get her talking. The one time I did, it sounded like when we were kids and our moms made us go to those plays at the civic center."

Walter Green took us through a tangle of vines and trees. "Isn't it kind of dark in here?" I whispered.

"Don't worry," George said. "I can still hear the freeway."

We came to a clearing where furniture had been dumped. Walter Green sat on a trashed sectional sofa. He dug into the earth with a broken china cup. He pulled up a whiskey bottle, and said, "Bourbon. Nearly full."

"Not for a million dollars," George said.

"All the more for me," Walter Green said. He unscrewed the bottle's cap and spilled drops of the bourbon into it.

George sat on a tire to watch his friend drink.

"My skin feels wet," Walter Green said eventually.

George handed the boy a Winston cigarette. I looked around in my purse for matches, but George had out a Zippo lighter, and the area suddenly smelled of lighter fluid.

George lit his friend's cigarette and then torched a spider-web, which we all watched frizzle.

I was thinking that I had been introduced and allowed to stay, but that I hadn't been invited into any real fellowship with these two.

From his wallet, George brought a folded page he opened. "My mom's fiancé," George said. "In England for that photograph." The page—ripped from a rock music magazine—showed Mack Armbruster.

"Quiet, I hear somebody," Walter Green said.

"It's only a jackrabbit," George said, but he slipped down

into the hole of his tire seat as he refolded the picture of Mack.

"Holy God!" Walter Green said, pointing at George's shoes. "I don't believe it. You're wearing your mom's penny loafers. I've seen them on her."

Walter Green laughed so hard he got off the sofa and onto all fours. He pounded his forehead against the ground.

"O.K., big deal. My sneakers fell apart in the clothes washer, so I'm wearing Lyla's shoes. What of it?" George said.

He moved sideways in the tire and tucked his feet behind a bush. He said, "Give me the whiskey, Walter. Since you aren't dead yet, I'll have some."

Walter obeyed, and George wet his lips and drank two or three swallows. He gasped, fanned his mouth, and rasped, "Give me the cigarette!"

"Did you swipe them from your dad?" Walter Green asked.

"I don't even have one," George said.

"Lie," said Walter Green.

"Look," George told him. "I no longer have a dad."

"Really?"

"Really," George said.

Because I was there as only a spectator, I didn't mention Jay.

⌐ With George trailing me, I followed the clack of a typewriter up to the attic. Uncle Ajax was hunched over his stand-up Adler. He spun on his chair to face us. He asked, "George. What was the last book you read? I need an idea for a title."

"Uh ... *Kidnapped*," George said.

"Couldn't be," said Uncle Ajax. "That was the last book you'd read the *last* time I asked you—three years ago."

"What're you typing?" I asked.

"I'm writing an autobiography, or more like a painting journal. I'm explicating each of my works, and I've penciled little sketches of them to include in the book. See?" Uncle Ajax showed me his drawings.

I said, "Wow, these are good. May I have this one, or a copy? To keep, I mean."

"I'm bored with you two," George said. "I think I'll go downstairs and start a fight with Lyla."

He did. We could hear George and Lyla, way below us in the kitchen, shouting and sometimes pounding the walls.

"You know, I've done some writing," I said to Uncle Ajax. "The fact is, I secretly wrote Jay's master's thesis."

"Yeah? Who doesn't know that secret?"

"It's that I'm rather proud of that particular work," I said. "In it, I completely defied the idea that man's the only creature who uses symbols. Chimps do, dolphins do. Hell, dogs do. Not that I care now. I now see the social sciences as a lot of hooey. They shouldn't even be called sciences. They're merely philosophies."

"I hate interrupting, but I must," Uncle Ajax said. "I have a three-layer cake in the oven that'll fall if those two keep banging."

When we got down to the kitchen, Lyla and George were still going at it—pacing, gesturing, glaring at each other. George picked up a water glass and pitched it at his mother, which she caught and held as she chased George into the living room.

Uncle Ajax and I followed.

George grabbed Lyla's Nikon from a shelf, and for a few seconds everyone's movements stopped. George lifted the camera high. His breath was coming fast. He seemed to be puffing himself up for the act.

"No you don't!" Lyla screamed, but weakly. Her voice was hoarse already from shouting.

George dropped the camera. Lyla whirled defeatedly and stomped out of the room and back through the kitchen. She flapped the rear screen door and ran barefooted down the lawn behind the house.

The three of us watched her from the doorway.

Lyla's quilted maternity robe flew behind her as she went.

"Look what you've done to your poor mother!" I said to George.

"Faith," he said, "I was defending you."

"Me?"

"Yes, ma'm," George said. "You'd think you'd show a little appreciation."

The shopping mall was crowded with back-to-school shoppers. Over the piped Muzak, George and Walter Green were arguing about an artificial palm at the entrance to the Holloway House, where we were on line.

"They're fireproof, moron," Walter Green said. "It's the law."

"I don't give a hell," George said. He huddled beside the potted palm. He put his Zippo lighter to a leaf. Fire rushed up and down the plant's structure until it was a three-foot figure of flame. An alarm sounded. Both boys ran off in the mall. I saw them duck into a Woolworth's.

Walter Green had a seat in Woolworth's phone booth by the time I arrived. The booth's glass door was folded open and Walter was saying, "The reason I can't go home is my brother. He's looking for me for taking his bike without asking." Walter listened to the phone for a minute. He said, "Sheila, thank you. Nobody'll know I'm there. I'll come over right away and bring you mascara and jewelry and stuff."

He hung up. I watched him proceed along the first aisle. He shoplifted a packet of pink disposable razors, a mini hair dryer, a foil-wrapped box of Mr. Bubble.

George and I wandered into the record and tapes area. George pointed to several of the albums under the "New Releases" marker. He said, "My mom has those. She has almost all of those."

Walter Green joined us. "We're in trouble. Ninth graders are here," he said.

"Oh, Jesus, your brother could be with them," George said. "Let's go to the bras and underpants. They won't look for us there."

Walter Green was waddling now from all the junk he'd stolen and hidden in his clothes. "I'd have done better if I'd had a coat and taken longer," he told me.

We were in the nylons section. A customer said to George, "All right, put back the panty hose."

"Why panty hose?" I asked as we were leaving.

"For Lyla," George said. "She is my mom."

"So what happens now?" I asked Lyla. It was the next afternoon, a Sunday. We were in the bright kitchen. Lyla was eating vanilla yogurt in the cold cast by the open refrigerator.

"With Jay? How would I know?" Lyla said.

I said, "Lyla. Think! What're you planning? Shouldn't you divorce Jay if you're going to have Mack's child?"

"Divorce handsome Jay? I hadn't considered it."

"Well, do so," I said. "Now."

Uncle Ajax came in and filled a ceramic mug with coffee from the Krups machine. His hands were spattered with gesso.

He reached into the refrigerator's freezer compartment and got out a Milky Way bar, which he ate, standing, at the high kitchen windows. He sipped his coffee, stretched onto tiptoes, and said, "There they go. Quitting. Before it rains." He meant the mowers who had been cutting Lyla's back lawn.

"What does Jay say about Mack and me? Does he talk about us?"

"Sure, all the time," I lied.

Uncle Ajax turned from the window. "Pancakes!" he said, and went around flapping cabinets, yanking out ingredients.

Lyla and I moved out onto the side porch to watch the oncoming storm.

"Damn it, look what those Escher twins did to my hedges!" Lyla said. She sat down.

After a moment, she said to me, "So it turns out you *do* want Jay after all."

"Oh, Lyla," I said, and shook my head at her: no.

The storm hit. Leaves turned up their white sides. Near the garage, two trash cans blew over. Lyla's maternity blouse winked in the changing light, and her sleeves flew out like wings in the terrible wind.

When the noise lowered some, I told her that I had a friendship with Jay and that it had been hard earned. I said, "We survived as friends because we both insisted. If you'd give your marriage half a try, it could do the same."

"Oh, pardon me, but how exactly was your and Jay's friendship hard earned?" Lyla asked. She leaned heavily back in her chair.

A siren sounded from about three blocks over. "Here it comes. Get ready," Lyla said.

"What for?" I asked.

Across the street, with the storm-darkened sky for a backdrop, several figures sprinted from the party house and ran off in different directions.

"That," Lyla said. Two black-and-white squad cars arrived.

One person remained on the second-floor balcony of the party house. "Go the hell away!" he yelled at the policemen.

We waited.

From behind the chopped hedges near us, a voice said, "O.K., let's stay put. The cops won't come over here. They don't care about Lyla or the fat girl."

Blushing, I left Lyla on the side porch. I went inside to the kitchen, where Uncle Ajax stood over the stove. He swatted the browned side of a flapjack in a frying pan. He stepped back from a little puff of steam.

"I was just brutally insulted," I said.

"About your weight," said Uncle Ajax.

"Yes."

He put down his spatula and used both hands to pull his ears forward. "Dizzy Dean!" he said, and smirked.

I snatched my handbag. I walked out the rear screen door, and without a goodbye to Lyla or George, I drove at top speed for Saratoga.

Mack Armbruster had taken over Jay's room at the Rip Van Dam while Jay was in the hospital. Mack and I rocked side by side in chairs on the hotel's front deck. We talked about what was best for Jay. We decided we should visit him.

We found him in the lounge of the psychiatric wing. We had a fakey exchange about how each of us was doing.

Mack had brought chewing gum and challenged Jay to a bubble-blowing contest. Together on a couch, they chewed their gum furiously, purposefully. They repeatedly turned their heads, showing each other the huge bubbles they were blowing.

A nurse came in and made both men dispose of their gum. She looked like a Gabor sister.

Jay said, "You know, I telephoned my old piano teacher. The guy didn't even know me, didn't recognize my name.

And to think of the nightmares I've had about him. The sheer number."

The nurse said, "You better have stranger dreams than that if you plan to stay long. There're plenty of cute guys running around with health insurance."

Mack Armbruster said, "I once dreamed all nine innings of a softball game."

"Well, I dreamt a chess match that took all night," I said, and both men turned to me as if I'd just arrived.

"May my friends go back to my room with me?" Jay asked the nurse.

"Yes, but you didn't hear me say yes," she said.

"I have a gift for you, Faith, in my room," Jay said. We headed down the hall. Jay said, "I specifically don't have a gift for you, Mack, because I still remember what you did to my dog. He *borrowed* my dog and renamed it Tina, which was all it would answer to ever after, though it was a guy."

Jay searched the clothes drawers in his room. He slid out a watercolor he'd done in art therapy. "What do you think, Faith? Is it worth framing?"

"Unequivocally yes," I said.

"On what grounds?" asked Jay.

"Uh," I said. "It's colorful?"

"Maybe you'll like this," Jay said. He produced a second drawing. This was a map of Texas with check marks and circles at various places. Texas was Lyla's home state, where her parents still were. Jay pointed to three of the check marks, saying, "I'd live there the rest of my days. Or there. I could contentedly live there."

Before I left with Mack, I said, "Jay, I think deep down Lyla really does love you."

"I know it. I'm counting on it," Jay said. "Remember what kind of gambler I am. I hardly ever lose."

. . .

Mack got his emerald green sports car from the hospital's parking garage. He told me he was meeting Lyla later, at a dance place called the Bijou.

I realized this wasn't an unhappy time for Mack.

We drove awhile. We stopped at a Shell station. Mack used the washroom while his car was getting fuel.

Climbing back behind the wheel, he said, "You ought to thank me, Faith. I did you the favor of erasing your name and phone number from the walls in there. Although I did leave the little limerick that's written about you."

The car was still taking gas from the pump. I hadn't smoked a cigarette in two years, but now I lighted one of Mack's Winstons.

"Jesus, put that out!" he said. "Didn't you ever see the movie *The Birds?*"

When we were moving again, I said, "You know, Mack, your number-one quality, and the chief thing everybody always liked about you, was that you kept to your own business."

"Lyla and the baby are my business," he said.

With all the attention on Jay, I had forgotten to notice how gently handsome Mack Armbruster was; how orderly were his features, how comforting his shadowy gray eyes.

"Of course, I still care for you," I said.

"You can't say that now," Mack told me.

"I am saying it," I said.

"Then I have to let you out, Faith. I can't have you talking that way."

Later, at my condo, I took on the task of explaining me to me. What I ached for was a repeat of a thing that had happened long ago.

The band was practicing in Mack's garage one evening. I went there. Mack's hair was longer then, and wavier; it curled on the back of his neck. He had on his wire-frame glasses, which he wore only when working. In those days, playing electric piano was working.

And never mind how conducive the circumstances, or what little had come before. I went there, where he was, and he looked at me with love.

MIRROR

Behind us were counters with cool basins and cabinets framed with white or amber bulbs. There was overhead, overbright lighting as well. And music—piped from somewhere above—to which Lolly kept time with her duck boot. We were side by side in swivel chairs, at a hair salon near the Watergate.

I asked Lolly what was so absorbing in her magazine—a young women's thing, with frantic announcements about dreams and skin tone on the cover.

"This asinine survey," she said indignantly. " 'What Women Want Most in a Man.' Can you believe it? Intelligence is ranked fourth here, behind security and good eyes. An athletic build is number one."

"Yeah, prizefighters," I said, and sighed happily.

"You're as bad as they are," Lolly said.

In the mirrors, my eyes looked fierce beneath straight black brows, which were like charcoal strokes. My lips are dark naturally, but here they looked stained by red wine.

"Hopeless," Lolly said with sudden affection.

Our heads were prickly with perm curlers. We were draped in blue plastic ponchos with fresh cotton shoulder bibs on top. Under her poncho, Lolly wore careful layers of expensive clothes. Her ears, with their gold dot earrings, were worried pink at the lobes. We are longtime friends. We went from kindergarten all the way through Potomac Senior together, in Baltimore. We graduated at the same time, four years ago. I live in Boston, but I'd been visiting Lolly in Washington lately, camping at her place in Foggy Bottom—a third-floor two-roomer on H Street.

"My head tickles," she said. "Is yours burning? I think they're making us keep our curlers in too long."

"Oh, yikes," I said.

Lolly ejected from her swivel chair, leaving it wiggling.

"Where are you going?" I said to her back.

She stalked across the deep main space and headed through one of the enameled doors at the back—the washroom, I guessed.

Aside from a few snipping sessions, I hadn't had my hair really cut since I was fifteen. I had kept it side-parted—a straight veil about my face. I didn't think my hair needed a professional to tangle it. Today's hair job was Lolly's idea and her treat. "To thin your hair, but give it a fluffier look, with more body," she told me severely. She knew I'd always preferred to mow my own split ends.

"Things in D.C. are all right—trustworthy, the best next to New York," she said. "You wouldn't let a Baltimorean *near* your hair." Since she'd moved to Washington, she took responsibility for everything about it. She was proud of this but embarrassed too.

Now I was looking around, panicky. The salon's walls had a pink-and-black wallpaper, with many gold French poodles descending a winding staircase. All the hairdressers were up at the front of the salon, in a conference of some kind. I tried to lose myself in Lolly's magazine. I went through it once and then, caught by nothing, started again with the first article: "Envy—What It Does to *You*."

This was Christmas season, a wintry day. The salon was full of noisy customers, chattering, knitting, thumbing paperbacks. More women arrived, in furs, mufflers, and galoshes. They carried shopping bags stuffed with varnished red paper and glinting foil. One woman I could hear was saying she had just spotted Baryshnikov over at the Star Market. "He was in floor-length sable," the woman said. "I swear it."

There was a blond child loose. She was two or three years old, dressed in a doll's version of the salon's livery—a tiny smock and nylon trousers. She came stumpily over to me and offered a round complexion sponge pad.

"My friend's missing," I told the little girl, who fitted the sponge into her mouth and left.

Lolly returned by and by. "Hi," she said cheerfully.

"Is it O.K. you didn't take out the curler rods?" I said. "That's good? It means our hair isn't getting scorched?"

"I was once here with my father," Lolly said absently. "I mean, here in D.C., of course. Father took me to dinner in Georgetown. This was over ten years ago, when we were in middle school. Anyway, Father saw John Mitchell in the restaurant where we were eating. Mitchell had been sick and he looked like the air had been let out of his face, although he was dressed in a very nice cashmere topcoat when he came in."

Lolly hoisted herself into her chair and swung sideways to face me. "Father said, 'Sweetheart, that's John Mitchell,' and I said, 'Who is John Mitchell?'"

"Was everything O.K., Lolly?" I said. "Are our heads all right?"

"Yeah," Lolly said. "On that same night, in the ladies' room in the same restaurant, written on the mirror there in crimson lipstick was 'If you're looking for the future, you're looking in the right place.'"

"Why is my scalp on fire?" I asked. I patted the spiky rollers. "What do I smell burning?"

"You won't believe this," Lolly went on, "but the same

woman just wrote the same thing in *this* washroom. Whoever she is. I mean, she could be here with us today."

Lolly and I peered around.

I said, "Seriously, Lolly, could something be going wrong with my hair? Am I going to come out of this with a Mamie Eisenhower?"

"Possibly," Lolly said. "I think I should have told them I'm pregnant. It can make a difference as to what chemicals they dump on you."

"I'm worried," I said.

Lolly was slumped low on her spine now. She stretched her legs and yawned expansively. "I was just kidding. You're completely fine," she said.

The hairdressers' team conference had broken up. A man with Inca features and a brown line of beard came over to us.

"All is well? Very bored?" he asked. He checked his gold wristwatch. The watch was nestled in several gold wrist chains. "Soon now," he said.

"Good, Kenny," Lolly said. Her eyes were closed.

"I'm glad I brought up the subject of the baby," she said when Kenny had drifted on. "What's your opinion of Doug, really?" Doug was the father. He and Lolly weren't married. They weren't even dating anymore.

I studied my fingers, frowning some.

"Come on, tell me—it's O.K.," she said. Her head bent forward. She was trying to get me to look at her. "He's not husband material, is he?"

"He wouldn't be for me," I said.

"So that's out," Lolly said. "One down, out of several big decisions."

"Do you *want* a child, here and now?" I said. "On your income?"

Lolly's job was clerical, at the Library of Congress.

"Next year I'll be a G.S. three," she said. "And besides, money isn't quite at issue, thanks to my folks." She had pushed back in her seat and thrown one long leg over the other. She was in the earnest posture of a talk-show host. "My mother and father could shelter us nicely and do a lot of the work, and they'd probably love it. The routine *and* the baby."

I was considering the other people in the shop. "Maybe the lipstick writer is one of the help," I said. "Maybe a manicurist."

"I think my father would especially enjoy a grandchild. My little sister would get to be an aunt."

"The help?" I said. "Did I just say 'the help'? See how you get me talking?"

"Two different worlds," Lolly said. She was mopey-sounding and hurt.

"I'm sorry. It's just—do you know how stupid I feel right now in this stuff? I can't discuss anything, looking like this, let alone something like your entire future life!"

Lolly seemed appeased. After a moment, she said, "I've thought about that lipstick message once a week, at least, every week of my life. And now here it is again."

"Well, people are funny," I said.

Lolly had reclaimed her magazine. She dabbed her thumb, with its steep lacquered nail, on her tongue and swished through pages. She said, "Yeah, like who'd guess from your appearance that you're a life model?"

A woman three chairs down tilted forward to stare at me.

"I would think that, even for some of those college guys, you're the first woman they've seen up close completely noodle," Lolly said.

One of my jobs is to model nude for the Francis Scott Key College adult-education evening art classes.

I put my hand on the razor ad in Lolly's magazine. "This is the last time I'll explain it to you," I said. "For me, the work is like an athletic event. It's an endurance test. For the students in the class, I'm a headache, an equation to be solved. I'm their homework."

"I know," Lolly said, and I could tell she wanted me to calm my voice.

"One guy actually said he wished I'd gain weight, so there'd be less anatomy to draw and more volume," I went on. "He said he does better with volume."

"Easy—just get pregnant," Lolly said.

I began to loosen my curler rods. "I want these out," I said.

"You cannot!" Lolly said. "They have a special way of removing those. You could end up bald."

The hairdresser, Kenny, hurried over. I was undoing the curlers and uncoiling damp squiggly hair. He started dripping neutralizer onto the curls I had undone. He said, "You pay anyway. I mean that emphatically."

"Attention!" I said to the room. "Who wrote that message on the bathroom mirror? Who of you here did that?"

We were going along Pennsylvania in a cab. Bits of snow, like flecks of paper ash, blurred the view. The avenue was hectic but festive with snow.

"You're not talking," I said.

"I'm so angry," Lolly said. Her lips were pursed. "You know I'm not a conformist, but still. Do you have to be so stubborn, always making a statement? I think of looking attractive as a favor to others. I do it out of respect for my fellow beings. It's considerate toward them."

I put a kind of half nelson on Lolly, who was horrified

until she realized I was being friendly—that the grip was an embrace. "When did you become a little teacup?" I asked her.

"I was paying for your new look," she said, laughing. "I wanted to see how you'd turn out."

The cab dropped me on H Street, at Lolly's apartment building. She was going off to lunch with Doug, to discuss her pregnancy and, more likely, to hear more about Doug's never-ending struggle to get graduated from G.W.

"I'm sorry," I said, leaning in through the open cab door to look at her.

"*You're* sorry," Lolly said. "Jesus, you just go back to Boston—problemless, unfettered. I'm here with nothing and no one, and I need so much help. I need you, for instance."

The cab took off abruptly, and I was left with the impression of Lolly's scared and beautiful face.

The lobby of her building had a lot of silvered glass, and marble the color of tangerines. I had forgotten to get Lolly's key, and I sat down in a waiting area on one of the cushioned pews that made a ring around a fountain. The fountain's bowl and cherub wore garlands of pine, and strands of Christmas bulbs were wound into the garlands. A tiny white nylon fir tree, hung with blue bulbs, stood in the corner between the switchboard closet and a wall of brass mailboxes. The switchboard area was watched by an attendant-doorman who had the looks of a wrestler. He had refused to take me up to Lolly's apartment and let me in.

I was glaring at him now, as I went into my second hour on the pew. "Come on, mister," I said.

He was reading a newspaper. His face had a burnt-red color, as if he had been out in the cold, which he hadn't. The ledge of his brow jutted out into a prominence that shaded his tiny eyes.

"Come *on*," I said. "You know me. You've seen me with Lolly a hundred times."

"You bother me again and I call the cops," the guy said. "It's not me locking you out, it's policy."

"You're a scary guy," I said.

I had gotten tired of my own reflection, which was coming at me from three directions. My hair clutched at my temples and neck; I couldn't get it to hang down. My substance seemed to have left me, and it was as though my body had become an armature supporting my coat and clothes. And I was hungry.

"You shouldn't be here anyway, this long in a private lobby," he said. "Go find yourself a grating. Outside."

I went through my wallet, discarding a visitor's pass to the Senate, which I'd never use, a note sheet of directions to someone's house near Rock Creek Park, and the worn end of an emery board. I let these things drop onto the rug by my shoe. With a pencil I made a few notes in the margin of a comic page in the *Post*, after I had read "Judge Parker" and "Rex Morgan, M.D." It was a little list about Lolly and me.

"Is that your mess?" the attendant said when he noticed. "I say to you, Is that your mess on the floor? Because I'm dialing the police." When he stood up he looked bloated. His belly sloped out well beyond the belt line of his uniform trousers. "For all I know, you're plotting a robbery," he said. "I don't want any company on my job here all evening. I'm working, see, no matter how it looks to you. If you belonged, you'd have a key. If you were supposed to be here, I'd know it."

With each of these pronouncements, I nodded my head yes or no, mocking him.

"I'm saying stop that. Fair warning."

I kept thinking of Lolly's apartment, just three floors above.

It was a beginner's place, mostly—neat and bookless. "I'm culturally bereft," Lolly had told me once. But there were fresh sheets, taut on her double bed. There was a glazed dish of Granny Smith apples on the Formica kitchen counter. There were draperies that Lolly had lined and sewn herself, from fabric she got at Laura Ashley. There was a clay pot containing a four-foot avocado plant. There was, on a shelf, a collection of stuffed pandas. Each bear was pristine; two were still in cellophane, and Lolly had displayed the boxes for the bears that came in a box.

I knocked off taunting the attendant and said, "So O.K., I'm sorry I bothered you. I'll pick up the papers."

"That's all I wanted, pick up," he said. "How am I supposed to know who you are?"

"That's true. And it's actually good that you're vigilant."

"Whatever that means," he said. "Are you sticking around for your friend? I have to know."

I was collecting the stuff from my wallet. I told him yes. I thought how his question and my answer had two meanings. I had decided—back in the cab, I realized—to stick around at least a little longer.

The list I made analyzing Lolly and me said that we were both waiting for something, that we had both been lucky and spoiled, and that we expected a lot. We thought alike sometimes. We remembered the same stuff. We were used to each other and could still be a help to each other. Of use.

I went over to the revolving doors. What snow there was had been chased from the street by the wind. A Federal Express truck slid up. The uniformed driver was rushing a package into the building across the street. The pink sodium-vapor light, from all the D.C. streetlamps, gave the sky a hopeful blush, as if it were not twilight.

ADORE HER

Steve was washing his car's headlights, pumping them generously with glass cleaner. He had parked the Saab in late afternoon shade on the old picnic green beyond the grounds of Baltimore's zoo.

His girlfriend, Chloe, had come along, and she had brought a small supper for them inside a rattan hamper. Chloe, at twenty-eight, was a little older than Steve. Her beach suntan was deep this June day. Her hair and eyebrows were sunlighted. She wore violet colors—a shorts and halter set. She had climbed onto one of the creaky picnic tables to sit. She looked so fetching there that the men nearby paused in their noisy poker game to watch as she leaned to pour iced tea or to scoop crab salad.

Chloe was the door hostess at an expensive eatery called La Lumière, down at the inner harbor. Whenever Steve caught sight of her in her work clothes, she had a look calculated to seem sprightly and alert, willing and ready. She had the suntan and, when that vanished, powder blusher across her cheeks. She wore tinted lip gloss, and blouses of sheer and vibrant fabrics under her well-tailored suits.

"Appearance is all," Chloe liked to tell Steve. "My job's not brain work. A cucumber could do it if it looked right and could endure."

Now, as Steve was stowing his paper towel roll and bottle of cleaning liquid in the Saab's trunk, he discovered a wallet lying on the sloped lawn behind the car. He waved away a yellow butterfly and plucked the wallet up out of the stiff grass. "Hey, anybody's?" he called. He shook the wallet for the poker players to see.

"What've you got, junior?" asked one of them.

"Billfold," said another.

"Ain't mine," the first man said. Two of them stood and patted their rump pockets.

"How much is in it?" Chloe asked.

"A couple singles and a five," Steve said. He took apart the wallet, which was new and cordovan leather. He turned up the inner flaps. There was an identification card and a hand-printed list inside, as well as a dozen photographs. "At least we've got a name," he said as he glimpsed the ID. "A Michael Gemini. And here's his address, and there're a whole lot of pictures of women included. There're ten or fifteen pictures. Some dress sizes or something written down here. No credit cards or driver's license. Nothing else."

Chloe said, "Hold it. Fifteen women, and the guy has only seven bucks? Is *his* picture in there? How about his telephone number?"

She was still up on the picnic table. She unwrapped a sandwich made on crustless bread. The poker men were being quiet, using the found wallet as an excuse to stare at her.

Steve hurried through the photographs, folded the wallet, and fitted it into the pocket of his khakis. The wallet made a square, high up on his right thigh. He frowned at Chloe, and said with mild displeasure, "No. There's no phone number."

He sat down on the picnic bench beside her bare, sun-polished legs.

"I've lost a million things, including a dog, and nobody's

ever gotten them back to me," Chloe said. "That Michael guy would be shocked and grateful if you'd give his wallet back safely to him. You really should, Steve," she said. She bit daintily at her sandwich.

Steve was trying to hate Chloe. He tipped his head to look at her from what he hoped would be a bad angle. For almost a year, he'd felt held hostage by his love for her. He had asked her to marry him many, many times. He had begged her.

"Why not? Why won't you?" he had asked.

Chloe never explained. "Poor kid," was the most she would offer as comfort after her laughing refusals.

He was seeing her now from close by and beneath, but no matter. She smelled of her sweet coconut tanning balm. She was much like the warm, flirty high school girls Steve had once dated and studied and learned how to please.

Often, these days, he allowed a fantasy. It was like a film loop playing itself over and over. In the fantasy, he and Chloe showered together, on a hot afternoon just such as this. They drank pink champagne and rode on the expressway in a white convertible afterward, and the wind threw Chloe's hair into a flamelike cone. Her tanned and freckled shoulders glinted, bare above a white strapless gown.

Chloe was saying now, "That dog I lost ran me like a machine! It got exactly what it wanted. It got food, walks, some of *my* food, you know? All by staring at me. Just sitting there and staring."

Steve considered the observing poker players, and decided he and Chloe had done enough picnicking.

They had apartments on different floors of the same Charles Street high-rise. Steve had introduced himself to Chloe in the underground parking garage there on an afternoon late last August.

He had taken her on a date soon after, to the races over at Pimlico. The two had found seats low in the bleachers, behind three uniformed Annapolis cadets. Chloe had brought along a pink nylon duffel filled with luncheon pastries— foods she'd bought at her workplace, La Lumière. The pastries, each wrapped in paper and aluminum foil, Chloe had passed all around and shared with everybody. She had worn cream colors that evening, and her perfume was a scent very like vanilla. "She's goddam cake icing," Steve had thought.

"All right, way to go, Lightfoot!" he had yelled when his choice of horse came in to win. "He is hot tonight!"

Chloe had said, "His jockey's sure darling."

"Oh, what do you mean, Chloe? You can't even *see* him."

"Honey, I see him," she had said. And Steve knew suddenly that Chloe looked assessingly at most men, most of the time, and that many men passed and came under her consideration, and the evening was ruined for Steve.

The day after Steve found the wallet, he was at his job, feeling restless and oddly outraged. He worked as a claims investigator for the Tidewater Assurance Company. He experienced now a revulsion for the job, thinking that in a lot of ways it involved tricking people out of money they were honestly due.

On a triple form, he marked: "Why not—just for once— *pay* this poor bastard?" He carved the letters with a hard-nosed pen, making scars through all three pages and their carbons. He stood and his ankle, which had fallen asleep, failed him. He dropped back onto his desk chair. He hesitated but pushed the forms into a manila envelope, which he waved above his head as though he were an auction bidder.

A woman named Iris soon appeared. She always wore an artificial iris pinned on her blouse or jacket lapel.

"I think we can all remember your name by now," Steve said to her, nodding once at the fake flower.

"Hand over whatever you've got to hand over," Iris said, and snapped the envelope from Steve.

Steve concentrated hard on Iris's hips as she maneuvered past rows of workers, but he could think only that her hips were not at all like Chloe's.

Iris delivered the envelope to Jerry Shevick, who was the senior adjuster. Shevick came straight around. "Are you putting me on, bud?" he asked Steve.

"I know," Steve said.

"No, seriously. Do you mean this? Because if you do, and you want your ass fired, that's fine and dandy with me."

"You're right, of course. A mistake," Steve said.

"This's your job," Jerry Shevick said, holding the envelope by an ear, but tightly. "I'm going to take lunch while you rewrite it, which you'd better do and do right, or *your* lunch break'll go on and on indefinitely."

"Shall do, sir," Steve said.

In his stark apartment after work, Steve still felt observed. He flicked the starter on the air conditioner and took a seat in his living room, which was well tended and had been decorated according to designer catalogues. He placed his attaché case on the brass-and-glass coffee table. He read most of the sweet-smelling *Baltimore Sun*, taking care to keep it in the air as he read, so as not to muss his summer suit. Steve realized he was being politely quiet, even though he was in his own home.

He threw the bundle of newspaper, got the wallet he'd

found from his attaché case, and looked—really seeing for the first time—at the wallet's many photographs. They were, some of them, just studio portraits of women, like yearbook photos. The lighting imposed on the faces and shoulders was cast too evenly. The backgrounds were vulgar red or painted scenes of baby-blue sky or midnight-blue darkness.

Two of the pictures had messages written on their backs. "Best love, Mimi," read one. Another woman, with popped eyes under not enough eyebrow, had penned: "The Future Mrs. Michael Gemini." "I'm afraid not," Steve told the photograph.

Several of the pictures were Polaroid shots, which had been trimmed to align with the others. The Polaroids had graphite tones—not true blacks and whites, but shades of stone and lead. These pictures were cropped to show only bodies of women in bikinis. The women were at least technically clothed, but the pictures seemed tasteless to Steve.

He sorted through the studio portraits again, trying to match the faces in those with the bikini-suited bodies in the others. He put the best face together with what he decided was the best body. He thought he could like this woman, if she were whole. But it was curious to Steve that anyone could have an interest in each of the women represented, however nice their figures or their smiles.

Chloe telephoned. She said, "Hallelujah!"

"Religion at last?" Steve asked, amused.

"No, better. I don't have to work tonight, so that means I have three days off in a row—three heavenly days."

While they talked, Steve trapped the telephone receiver between his shoulder and his strong jaw, and tucked away the wallet photographs.

"You sound kind of spent," Chloe said.

"*You* sure don't," Steve said.

"I'm partying already, friend. I earned it. You want to come to my party? We could also invite the guy whose wallet you stole."

"You say what? I stole?"

"Well, didn't you?" Chloe asked.

"Anyway," Steve said, "it isn't a real wallet. It seems more like an auxiliary wallet—the man's love file or something."

"So you assert."

"Listen, I do investigations for a living. That's what I do; what I have to do, not just smile, look chic, and dress well. And look fabulous, and smell like sugar and spice."

"Thank you," Chloe said.

"Well, I'm taking it back tomorrow."

"Your compliments?"

"No, girl, the wallet!" Steve said.

"If you go to do that, could I go with you?" Chloe asked.

On his lunch break the next afternoon, Steve drove alone to the address typed on the wallet's identification card. He had to use a road map he kept clipped to his sun visor to find the street called Key's Way.

"This can't be right," he said when he got to the neighborhood, which was suburban, with expensive old homes, all enormous and set well apart on three-acre lots with landscaped lawns and gardens. Number 70 was a long house made of quarry rock. The home had picture glass and was hidden behind a screen of rosebushes with fluffy white blossoms. Three sprinkler machines tossed ropes of water onto the brilliant front lawn. In the asphalt driveway sat a fairly new Mercedes.

Steve kept his own car idling by the hot curb. He checked his mirrors, outside and in. He wanted to read his face and confirm his good appearance in such a neighborhood. His reflection assured him. His shirt had a tasteful weave. His tie was discreet—red with a pin-dot decoration. He was glad that his Saab was tended perfectly. Its white upholstery still shone from the buffing he had done.

"More than acceptable," Steve said to himself.

He opened the catches on his attaché case. On a blank notepad, he wrote:

Dear Mr. Gemini,
    Here is the wallet you evidently misplaced. I did not look inside it except to ascertain your address.

On a new piece of notepaper, Steve wrote:

Dear Michael G.,
    Here's your wallet. Should you ever hear from a girl named Chloe, stay entirely away from her or you'll sure be sorry. I'm an investigator.

He balled up both notes and wrote a new one:

Michael Gemini,
    You have a lot of gall carrying these pictures around with you. And if you're going to, then you should never be so stupid as to lose your wallet. You're one careless son of a bitch.

Steve noticed a woman now standing behind the front door of number 70. The woman seemed just a plump shape, grayed over as she was by the shadowy glass of the storm door.

"That has to be his mother," Steve said. "Or it could be his wife. If it's his *wife* ..."

The Saab's engine made a pleasant burbling noise. Steve

checked the time. "Well, my lunch break's up. I better do something," he said. He plunged in the clutch, set his car in gear.

The woman raised a hand over her eyes.

"O.K., lady," Steve said. He drove the circle, using his right hand. In his moist left, he clasped the wallet. He opened it over his lap and flicked out every one of the photographs. He brushed them onto the Saab's floor, but challenged by the eyes in the rejected pictures, he said, "I'm doing nothing illicit. I'm trying to do Mr. Gemini and maybe his marriage to someone who might just happen to love him for some foolish reason a favor. I *could* just drop the wallet, bathing beauties and all, into a mailbox."

As Steve repassed number 70, he shagged the wallet through his car window. It was a good toss. Spinning, the wallet sailed uplawn and landed about halfway to Michael Gemini's door, halfway to the curious stubby woman behind it.

On the trip home, Steve stopped but left his car running. He shredded all the photographs, and walked determinedly to feed their pieces to a dumpster behind a hardware store.

Chloe was eating from a cardboard cup of banana yogurt. She seemed more interested in the yogurt and her dainty spoon than in Steve, who was visiting her in her apartment. Rain bubbled and splattered on her living room's north-wall windows. It was a storm cloudy Thursday, at the end of Chloe's holiday. Steve could tell that Chloe was dispirited and suffering a hangover.

As for the bottles of dark British beer Steve had brought along, she said, "Just keep those well away from me. I don't even want a whiff of them."

He studied Chloe. He tried to listen to only what he thought, not felt, about her. Her shapely legs and large breasts and pretty skin were lovely, but they seemed a mild embarrassment to her in her present flat mood. Her face was innocent, especially now when her suntan was diluted in the apartment's light and her small features weren't shaded with makeup.

He had been mistaken to expect or ask much from her, and he swore to himself that he wouldn't anymore. Chloe didn't owe him marriage, and he'd have to proceed as if—as in the wallet photographs—Chloe's substance were separate from Chloe's self. He would enjoy the body of Chloe, but he wouldn't try to possess the real her.

As honest as Steve was being, he recognized that his thinking was merely another temporary phase of his love. He suspected that sometime he'd be asking of Chloe, wanting from her, and that whatever she gave she would hand down to him—a concession.

So he said, "Drink to me."

"For?" she asked.

Eventually Chloe went to the kitchenette. She got a frosted glass from her compact freezer's shelf. She twisted open one of Steve's British beers and poured. When her glass was filled, she held it up and tapped it to his. "What the hell, here's to you," she said.

Steve had decided that as soon as Chloe finished drinking the one beer, he would leave. He would leave and he would run; run from the unalterables: from Chloe, the apartment building, Baltimore, his job at Tidewater Assurance. He'd run from everything he couldn't change about what he'd been calling his life.

I GET BY

Right after the windup of the memorial service in the hospital chapel that evening in February, the principal of the elementary school where my husband, Kit, had taught approached me. Enough of a crowd had gathered and passed that I had to inch over and strain to hear him, because the chapel doors had opened. From down the hall there were metal bed and tray noises, buzzers and dings, and doctor-paging voices, as my husband's mourners made their exit.

My mother-in-law, Rennie, still sat in the pew behind me, arm-rocking the baby, who was sounding little pleas. The principal was talking to me. "I think I've found a replacement for Kit," he said.

I had to let that remark hang there for a beat. He meant another teacher. He was either too cruel or too vacant a person to have prefaced what he'd said in some way. He told me, "Her name's Andrea Dennis. Came down from Danbury for interviews this afternoon. Knocked us sideways, actually. You two might get in touch."

I said, "Isn't that nice."

My kids, Ben and Bibi, helped me up from the pew. The principal mentioned he'd tried to call with his condolences. Possibly he had; I had unplugged all three of our phones.

After we got home, Ben and Bibi lingered in the backyard. It was snowing by now—a friendly snow, scurrying in the floodlights behind the house. Rennie took over the couch. She had the baby and our whole stack of pastel sympathy cards. "Going to *read* these," she said, as though someone ought to do more than open the envelopes and nod, acknowledging the signatures.

I warmed a bottle of formula in hot tap water, and watched my children through the window over the sinks. Bibi had fitted into the tire swing somehow. She is broad-bottomed at eighteen. The swing's rope, knotted around a limb of the weeping willow tree, was stiff with ice.

Ben was only a few feet away, urinating onto a bump of snow. I had to look twice, to be sure. He was eleven, *almost* eleven, and peeing in view of his sister.

Bibi had just colored her hair, but I wasn't ready to accept her as a champagne blonde yet. She looks *familiar*, I'd think, whenever I happened onto her.

The Saturday morning we learned about Kit, the Old Hadham police visited. So did two station wagons from television news teams. I took a confirming call from the idiot aircraft-company people who'd rented Kit the light plane in which he died. After the call, I snapped the telephones out of their plastic jacks, and Bibi chain-locked the door of the upstairs bathroom and stripped away the hair color nature had given her.

I met Andrea Dennis. I was at the school, sorting through two decades' worth of teacher paraphernalia, looking for anything personal in classroom cupboards and in Kit's mammoth oakwood desk. I found a comb, his reading glasses, a Swiss Army knife, and a hardback copy of *Smiley's People*, bookmarked halfway. This was on a school day, but after classes had adjourned. Andrea pushed open the heavy door and found me. She introduced herself in an inquiring way: "I'm Andrea?"

We talked some. We didn't say anything I thought to commit to memory. I spilled Elmer's Glue-All all over. The white glue moved thickly across the desk blotter. "I'd better take care of that," Andrea said. "Let me fetch a sponge or something from the lounge."

I used to be entirely comfortable in the staff and faculty lounge.

Old Hadham Elementary had gone up in '64. Inside and out, the building was an architectural oddity. Kit's classroom (he'd had half of sixth grade), for instance, was in the shape of a semicircle. His huge desk and his roller chair faced out from the straight wall. The room had three rising rows of student chairs with attached laminated writing arms. The floor was covered with jewel-blue linoleum. The curved wall wore a band of pale corkboard.

In the couple of weeks Andrea Dennis had been teaching, she'd tacked up stuff for the lull between Valentine's Day and St. Patrick's Day. There were pen-and-ink drawings that looked like student self-portraits to me. Some printed quotes were pinned up—sayings of statesmen and explorers. There were two science charts: one explaining the pollination of a flower, the other an illustration of polar and equatorial weather movements. Left over from Kit's days here were the usual flags—Old Glory and the Connecticut state flag—and some empty hamster cages with empty water fonts and play wheels. I planned to leave all those behind, of course, as well as Kit's globe, showing the continents and oceans in their proper cloudy colors. Kit hated globes with countries done in pink or purple.

I had to admit Andrea Dennis was an appealing woman.

She had clearly put a lot of clever thought and effort into presenting herself at her best. She had on a touch-me-please cashmere sweater and a soft wool-blend skirt with a lining that rustled. Her sheer nylons gleamed. She had hair long enough to toss.

I had noticed something about us. Whenever I mentioned Kit, I nodded at his desk. When Andrea referred to him once, she gestured north. Toward the forest where the plane fell?

I hung around for fifteen minutes. Andrea didn't return with the sponge. Anyway, the glue had hardened by now. I pictured her yakking away with young Mr. Mankiewicz or flirting with old Mr. Sonner.

I packed Kit's things into a blue nylon gym bag. I bundled up and walked home—a matter of a mile or so—in the road. My part of Connecticut has no proper sidewalks. I kept stumbling. Ever since the baby, and then especially after what happened to Kit, I had been sleeping sporadically and then only in short spurts. That was part of the reason I'd been so clumsy and had flubbed with the glue. My getup was pretty cockeyed too. I had forgotten to wear socks, and yet the shoelaces on my Nikes were triple-bow-tied. Beneath my parka, my sweater was lumpy and had the smell of Johnson's baby products, as did the whole interior of our beautiful saltbox house when I got there—baby oil, baby powder, baby's softened-fabric bunting.

Everywhere I looked was bright with baby things, baby artifacts.

I went into the kitchen, grateful for Rennie, who'd tidied up. Rennie had almost never stayed with us when Kit was alive. We'd seldom gone to see her. She lived alone on what once had been an apple orchard, near Darien. She cared for the big central house there, and there were two barns and two brown outbuildings on the land.

Her husband had long ago put himself into a VA hospital. He was a troubled, haunted man. I had witnessed some behavior. He'd sit for long afternoons with his head in his hands. He would roam searchingly over the yards and meadows. He'd seem to hide beside the shadowy brown barns. Other times, he'd pitch and splatter hard apples furiously against the fallen-in stone walls around the borders of the orchard.

Thinking of him, I made a bet with myself I hoped I wouldn't win. I bet that Rennie connected Kit's accident with his father's illness. That would have been unfair.

March came. We'd get a couple more snowstorms in Old Hadham, I suspected. Spring wouldn't arrive in any decided way for weeks and weeks. But I was seeing new grass and there was dry pavement. April would be breathtaking along our road. There'd be arbutus, hepaticas, downy yellow violets. In the living room, Rennie had sections of the local evening newspaper strewn around. The baby was in the playpen, wadding and tearing a Super Duper coupon page.

"Where's the baby's dolly?" I asked Rennie.

She said, "Ask Ben."

"Ben? Ben has Susie Soft Sounds?" But I didn't call up to Ben. Every day, it seemed, there was more about him and Bibi that I didn't care to know.

They had identical rooms, across the hall from each other —identical except that Bibi's wallpaper showed jazz dancers against a mint-green background, whereas Ben's had ponies grazing in a field. The night before, I had happened past the rooms and heard Bibi say, from behind Ben's door, "I am safely buzzed." Next I heard the pop-tab of what I assumed was a beer can.

"That's your *third*!" Ben had whispered.

Another curious moment was when I noticed something in among Bibi's hand laundry; she had borrowed my push-up bra.

Bibi talked a lot about Andrea Dennis these days. Andrea, it turned out, sometimes snacked after school at the Nutmeg Tea and Sandwich Shop, where Bibi waited tables. It seemed as if Andrea was always with someone I knew well, or had known. I could never resist saying, "Really? What did she have on? Did she look tired? Who picked up the check? Did they have desserts or entrees? Did she have that fruit cup?"

I was driving home with Rennie and the baby. We'd been to the lawyers'. The airplane company's insurance people had investigated and decided to settle some money on me. I liked it about the money, but what I wanted just now was my bed, pillows, the electric blanket. For three days, a quiet sleet had been falling on Old Hadham.

The car's windshield wiper on my side suddenly locked taut on a diagonal. A film formed immediately on the glass. I tried the squirters, but all I got was blue fluid congealing with the ice at the base of the windshield. I maneuvered down Willow, on Old Hadham's steepest hill—a plunger, which had been only cursorily sanded. There was a car not far ahead, and a truck on my tail, no shoulder. I had to tip my head out the driver's window to see. Meanwhile, Rennie was smiling, half asleep. The baby said a noise very much like "Why?" I had something close to nausea suddenly: suddenly missing Kit.

The baby woke me. It was an April morning, predawn. I was groggy, but I had a sweet dream still playing in my head—some of the dream's color and its melody—as I heated water for the formula and started coffee. "Here we come!" Rennie said, and drove the baby's castered crib into the kitchen. Rennie was oddly cheerful, giddy. Her taffeta robe was on inside out. She sat down and swayed the crib and sang some ballad about whaling boats and messmates, with a line about the lowland sea.

To distract the baby, Rennie had dropped a fat nest of pink excelsior into the crib—a leftover from Easter baskets. I was a little afraid the baby would eat the pink cellophane, so I intended to snatch it away. But for now the excelsior ball rolled back and forth with the crib's movement, and with Rennie's song and what rhythms there were of my lingering dream.

When the baby was asleep, we two sipped coffee. I figured Rennie would be stepping out onto the porch for sunrise, as she sometimes did, but instead she said she wanted to talk about her son, about Kit. I told her what I knew was true— that his character faults included overconfidence and impulsiveness. I said that he had taken all his lessons and received his license. But whatever the license signified, he hadn't been ready, not competent, to solo pilot a plane.

A lot of Old Hadham showed up at Chicwategue Park for Memorial Day. Some people brought picnic dinners and thermoses or coolers of drinks. The high school's brass-and-drum corps was there. There were two burros roped to a post for the little kids to ride around a guided circle.

Chicwategue Park had ducks on a pond, and a pair of swans—the town favorites—who'd made it through the winter, and bronze statues of Revolutionary War generals, and, in the center, a white-painted, lacy-looking gazebo. On the soccer fields beyond the woods, there would be footraces and other competitions throughout the day. Rennie had given Ben a two-year-old boxer she'd purchased through a newspaper ad, and Ben had entered himself and Reebok in the Frisbee contest.

I set up camp with the baby on a faded quilt. Rennie took Bibi to gamble away some of her waitress tips from the Nutmeg at the bingo tables. Watching them go, I noticed Andrea Dennis over by the penny-toss place—sporty and pretty in spotless sky-blue sweats, with a balloon on a ribbon looped at her wrist. She and Bibi greeted each other like classmates, with a hug.

Bibi's appearance looked to me like a screaming-out-loud reaction to Andrea Dennis. Bibi had whacked her fake-blond hair into bristles and points, and her face was dusted with chalky makeup. Her lips looked almost black, and the tank top and jeans she wore were black. Still, Andrea was giving Bibi approving looks and nods.

But if Bibi's getups scared people, at least her manner had improved. That morning at breakfast, I'd overheard her saying to Ben, "Relax and sit still. I'll fix you a fresh glass of orange juice."

Now Ben's name was called over the PA system. I carried the baby and trailed Ben and Reebok to the starting stripe on the Frisbee competition field. Ben had the dog's collar in one hand and his yellow Frisbee in the other. Ben was down on one knee and the dog was trembling with excitement as they waited for the judge's signal to begin their routine.

At the whistle, the dog bolted away down the field. Ben stood up and let fly. His first couple of tries were long, too fast throws, and the Frisbee sailed yards over Reebok's head. The dog wasn't paying attention anyhow. On their third and last turn, Reebok watched as he ran, then leaped, fishtailed, and chomped the disk, but only after it had ricocheted twice off the dirt. At the gazebo, the Frisbee judge held up a card, giving Ben and Reebok a "4" rating.

Andrea Dennis strolled over to us. She introduced herself to the baby and sort of shook hands with him. Ben and the dog came over. Ben's young face was bright, but I couldn't tell if it was from excitement or embarrassment.

Andrea said, "Man, you got robbed! Your dog flew six feet straight up. What do they *want?* They should've given you guys a special award."

Ben absorbed this. I knew that on the car ride home he would relive Reebok's last effort for Bibi and Rennie. He'd say he got robbed.

I asked him to watch the baby a minute—to make sure the kid didn't crawl away, go swimming after the swans, or filch anyone's barbecued spareribs.

I clapped a hand on the smooth blue sweatshirt material on Andrea's shoulder.

"What did I do?" Andrea said, and I said, "A lot."

We walked along together by the rows of blankets and the outdoor furniture that bordered the competition fields. We said hello to people—fellow teachers of Andrea's, the families of some of her students, old friends of mine.

I was thinking how to tell her that she had been an important distraction for me—maybe even a necessary one. She'd been someone safe for me to focus on while the reality of having no Kit was so fierce. I realized I couldn't make my interest in her into anything polite or easy to explain. I said, "Generally, thanks, Andrea," and I told her how great she looked in blue.

A NOTE ON THE TYPE

The text of this book was set in a digitized version of Fournier, a typeface originated by Pierre Simon Fournier *fils* (1712–1768). Coming from a family of typefounders, Fournier was an extraordinarily prolific designer both of typefaces and of typographic ornaments. He was also the author of the celebrated *Manuel typographique* (1764–1766). In addition, he was the first to attempt to work out the point system standardizing type measurement that is still in use internationally.

The out of the typeface named for this remarkable man captures many of the aspects of his personality and period. Though it is elegant, it is also very legible.

Composed by
Crane Typesetting Service, Inc.,
Barnstable, Massachusetts

Printed and bound by The Haddon Craftsmen, Inc.,
Scranton, Pennsylvania

Designed by Claire M. Naylon